I0716111

EXPLOITATION

NEON
BOOK FIVE

ALLYSON LINDT

ACELETTE PRESS

For my eternal dragon

CHAPTER 1

BRAGI

A famous bard once said *don't know what you got, till it's gone. Don't know what it is I did so wrong.*

It was unlikely anyone but me would remember who Tom Keifer was, a hundred years from now, but I would. Because despite having lost all my power—my innate sense of what the people around me were feeling, the ability to create pocket realities and blink from one place to another—I still had my immortality.

At least if I got hurt, I still healed instantly.

The loss of most of my power was why I was standing on a street corner in Chicago Underground, staring at a building with no windows or doors. How was I going to get in?

I couldn't. That was the problem. I *knew* the entrance was here. I'd visited NEON plenty in the last few decades. But now that I was *persona non grata*, the owners' magic kept me from seeing the place.

There was one thing to be grateful for when it came to losing most of the abilities associated with my godhood. Every time someone brushed past me on the street, each of the dozens of people milling around me like I was one of them, I didn't feel what they were feeling.

It was like losing my sense of hearing or sight, but at least the pain of human suffering vanished with it.

Intellectually, I knew that inside, it was a massive high rise, thanks to magic that allowed doors here to open to different buildings in other places. Outside was a nondescript one story building.

No. Really. The charms on it made it so that I forgot what it looked like the instant I turned away.

Frey—Freyr, the god of passion who claimed this place as his realm—had doubled down to make sure I couldn't find who I was looking for.

I had to, though. I needed to speak to Magnus, because of the loss of my power. The prophecies were clear about why this had happened to me...

Okay, not quite. The prophecies were *never* clear. But this one was about me, and I'd studied it for centuries, and I had some educated guesses about what it meant. The fact that I was impotent was an indicator that something bad had happened to Nico, and worse was about to happen to Magnus.

Something bad was vague, but welcome to the wonderful stories told by ancient dragons who were more interested in entertaining themselves than in writing their visions down in minute detail.

Not that I blamed them. The story should always come first.

Almost always. In this case, I hated that I didn't know what I was up against or how to save the people I loved. The beings I missed so terribly it ached in every inch of me. For decades, I ignored how I felt about Nico, the phoenix I'd known for centuries. He walked away from me when I sided with the gods who were trying to keep things like losing my powers from happening.

I wanted to go to him now. Help him. Save him.

I couldn't. My passport was expired, because why the fuck would I need to keep that current, when I had the ability to blink from place to place in an instant?

Which was why I was standing in front of where NEON was supposed to be instead. Magnus was here. I couldn't feel her, but she wouldn't go anywhere else.

So I'd walked into an airport with a bookstore full of the most generic books humanity had to offer, gotten on a plane, flown across the United States surrounded by screaming children and chatty people.

If I shouted Magnus's name over and over again, would I get the desired response? Or would I land myself on a series of videos online, and earn a night in jail as a reward?

A new person—another god—appeared in front of me.

"You're not welcome here." Frey was lithe, with hair that flowed in blond tresses, and a presence that radiated sensuality. The kind of being people used to write ballads about. Maybe that Cinderella song was about him. "Though, you already know that."

This was all the opening I needed. "Let me talk to Magnus."

His appearance was deceptive. The power he held could raise nations. "You're lucky I didn't let someone else come out here."

"I'm surprised you didn't." If I were to encounter Dahlia, a dragon, or Fen—Fenrir—a massive wolf god whose historical favorite pastime was ripping enemies to shreds with his jaws for fun—either would kill me without hesitation. Or try. That whole *healing instantly* thing sucked when one was being repeatedly injured. "In fact, I don't know why you're speaking to me."

Frey dragged in a deep breath and his nostrils flared. "You told me how to save Fen. My repayment to you is letting you leave today with your life."

It was probably a fair offer. I wasn't going to take it. "I want to see Magnus. Let me do that, and I'll go."

"You don't seem to understand; you have no power to make demands here."

I had no power, period. But that was a secret between me and the fictional characters in my head. As far as anyone else knew, I was as powerful as I'd ever been. "I could stand here until you comply."

"I could send you to Antarctica." It seemed Frey had supplemented his negotiating tactics with some of Dahlia's skills. That retort wasn't like him.

"I'd just come back."

Frey narrowed his eyes and studied me. "Would you?"

I would not. Not instantly, anyway. Given a few weeks, and enough luck to stumble on some sort of expedition or research center, I could charm my way onto a boat, and be back here in about a month. "No. I'd take vacation in the frigid weather and freeze my cock off." I let the sarcasm drip into my voice. "What kind of question is that?"

"I've got this." Magnus's voice came from behind me.

No one on the street cared that two individuals had appeared from nowhere. But I did. Hearing her voice made my heart race, despite her frigid tone. Not long ago, I would've felt the antipathy radiating from her. Been bathed in her scorn before she even spoke. Even when she hated me, the feelings she radiated were intoxicating.

Now, I couldn't sense so much as a whiff of disdain.

She was here, though. I turned to face the assassin-turned-Valkyrie. The woman with the auburn curls pulled away from her face, and the fury of a thousand armies flashing in her emerald-green eyes. She was more stunning than any goddess. Stronger. More alluring.

"Magnus." I loved the way her name tasted on my tongue.

"Will you be all right?" Frey asked her.

She looked past me. "If he's going to suffer, I want it to be by my hand."

She hated me because I'd lied to her. Because I'd let her believe her sister was dead, to keep Magnus safe. I'd do it again in a heartbeat. She was a creature like no other, and I'd let the world burn to keep her from harm.

"I could send out Fen," Frey said.

That would suck, if Fen decided I was his plaything for the night.

"No." Magnus flexed her fingers, and the lamplight glinted off the claw ring on her middle finger. The ring was made from one of Dahlia's claws, which granted Magnus a handful of potent, dragon-like powers. Magnus had dark circles under her eyes, and the longer I studied her, the more apparent her exhaustion was. "I've got this, really. Thank you."

"We're only a shout away, if you need," Frey said.

A glance over my shoulder told me he was gone again. Good.

I turned to Magnus and reached for her, barely registering that was what I was doing.

She stepped back with a scowl.

I expected a wave of hate and loathing, but it wasn't there. Or rather, I couldn't feel it. I was grateful as fuck that I hadn't had to feel the emotions of everyone on the plane, but losing a sense was debilitating.

I needed her to hear me out, not just because I missed her. The prophecies said—heavily implied—that when I lost my power, it would be because the people I loved were in danger. Something had happened to Nico; every instinct I had insisted as much, even without my power.

I needed to reverse that, and make sure worse didn't happen to Magnus.

The problem would be, getting her to hear me out, and believe me on top of that.

"What's wrong with you?" Magnus furrowed her brow and tilted her head.

The question didn't sound like the sort of angry thing shouted during an argument. It wasn't a frustrated scream of disbelief. This was more curiosity.

"I miss you." That was a good starting point.

"Are you here to beg forgiveness?"

"No." Because I hadn't done anything wrong.

She winced and shook her head, then turned away.

Nothing about her expressions and posture were what I expected, but that didn't mean I was letting her leave before we finished this conversation. I grabbed her arm.

The grunt she let out was filled with pain, and she stumbled, jerking away from my touch as she fell to her knees.

"The fuck did you just do to me?" She gasped out the words.

Nothing. I wasn't capable of it. What happened to her?

CHAPTER 2

MAGNUS

When Bragi touched me, emotions that weren't mine flooded me. I'd sensed hints the instant I appeared in behind him, but I figured it was because he was radiating extra ick.

But the moment he put a hand on me, I was overwhelmed by rage. Desire. Worship. Adoration. Concern. Self-loathing.

Okay, that last one might be mine, but I usually suppressed it better than that.

The wash was potent enough that I stumbled. Landing on my knees jarred me back into my own head.

"Are you all right?" Bragi knelt next to me.

I crawled back from letting him touch me again, and the people on the sidewalk muttered strings of *watch out* and *idiotic girl*.

One of the passersby kicked me, and the disgust and disdain roared in my thoughts.

What. The. Fuck?

I dragged in a deep breath, trying to focus myself, and stood, refusing to let him touch me again. "I'm fine."

"I'm surprised you came out to talk to me," he said.

Yeah, well... I had a secret he didn't get to know. Namely that I was pregnant. And because it was a supernatural kind of thing, one of the babies was his and one was Nico's. "I can't believe I'm saying this, because there's no way I can trust most of what you tell me, but... I need to know everything you do about Nico."

Because about a month ago, Nico died, giving me time to escape from the god who wanted me dead. Since Nico was a phoenix, he came back. Neat trick. Would've been an even better one if his memories had come back with him.

"You'll need to be more specific than *tell me everything*," Bragi said. "But I'll answer your questions."

Uh-huh. As in, he'd tell me what he felt I needed to know, and leave out the rest. I'd have to do a lot of reading between the lines.

This was one of those times I was begrudgingly grateful for my upbringing. I'd been raised by a group of gods who believed they could evade the dragons' prophecies. Those gods taught us to hunt and more on their behalf, to eliminate the threats that could destroy them.

I knew an implausible number of ways to kill. I'd also been taught how to seduce information out of people, and understanding subtext had to be second nature. Not only to find what I was looking for, but to evade punishment from our *mentors*.

Sometimes it was exhausting looking for hidden meaning in everything, but with Bragi it would be necessary. Especially if he sensed my wariness with those fucking empathic abilities of his, and countered before I realized that he'd reacted.

"I give you my word, that as long as I know the answer, and Nico hasn't sworn me to secrecy, I will tell you." Bragi used his finger to trace an X over his heart.

That was a lot of detail up front, which made me suspicious, but it would have to do. "Can we go someplace public and talk? Sit? Eat?"

"There's a coffee shop down the street."

I was familiar with it. Dahlia and I walked down there a lot. Both for the caffeine and to pretend we were normal, as opposed to two orphans who had somehow acquired immense power in our early thirties, and could take on most gods without batting an eye.

I was surprised Bragi suggested it, though. That he didn't try to convince me to travel halfway around the world with him to some remote, exotic location. I was also a little concerned that he knew this area well enough to suggest a nearby coffee shop, though I could chalk that up to him noticing it when he blinked into this location.

"That sounds good." I fell into step beside him, but kept enough space between us to avoid touching him.

The thing I hated more than anything about this was the pull I felt to him. He was a gorgeous man with light brown hair that was just long enough to curl around his collar, and piercing eyes. When he wanted it, a gift for words, and yeah, there was something appealing about the fact that he would kill for me.

I was still furious at him for lying to me about Dahlia. For locking me up for a month.

But he'd healed me when I thought I'd lost my power. He took care of me. None of that was enough to splash green on red flags, but part of me still wanted him.

As we walked, I kept getting snatches of feelings I didn't recognize. Like a scent on the wind that I couldn't quite identify before it vanished again.

Being surrounded by so many people was both comforting and disconcerting. Bragi didn't tend to be an in-my-face kind of scary, but there was safety in numbers, right? On the other hand, he was a god. I was being hunted by gods. There was no one here who could stop one if my pursuers came after me, and no way for me to know if a god or one of their servants was walking next to me.

Thanks for the rampant paranoia, Life, I don't know what I'd do without it.

Stepping into most any coffee shop was comforting to me. There was an aura of warmth that encased us, and few scents promised security better than freshly roasted and ground beans.

Great, now I was getting all poetic. The last thing I needed was Bragi rubbing off on me.

There weren't many other customers, and the woman behind the counter looked up the moment we walked in. She gave us a warm smile. "Good afternoon."

Bragi approached her without hesitation, as if it wasn't necessary to do a visual sweep of the entire room. Fortunately I knew the layout from past visits —where the knickknack shelves were, the tables, and the alternate exits—but other patrons and employees always had to be assessed and stored on top of the mental blueprint.

"Hi there." Bragi was as friendly as the woman. "I'll have a macchiato, and she'll have a white chocolate mocha and a blueberry muf—"

"Whoa." Was that presumptuous asshole ordering for me? "You do *not* get to order my food."

The woman's smile faltered. "What can I get you?" She looked at me.

Damn it. How did he know? "White mocha, blueberry muffin." My reply was sheepish. I wanted to be defiant and order something completely different, but now nothing else sounded good.

Fortunately, Bragi kept his smugness to himself. "No, not that one." He stopped her as she reached under the glass display case. "The one next to it has more blueberries."

I didn't protest when Bragi paid the bill. In my experience, money didn't mean much to most gods, since they'd seen so many constructions of it rise and fall over the centuries, and most had more than they knew what to do with.

On the other hand, the pay for an out of work assassin—me—crashing in her sister's boyfriends' magical condo wasn't great.

Besides, it was my understanding that Bragi acted as his own estate for the works he'd published under various pen names throughout the centuries. Given that CS Lewis's estate just sold the movie rights to the Chronicles of Narnia *again* I was going to assume he could afford ten or fifteen bucks for a nosh and a drink.

We had our pick of tables, and I chose one with the best view of everything. Being out in the open like this with someone I didn't trust made my skin crawl, but with him, the idea of being alone made me uncomfortable, too.

I kept a shield around us—a magical, protective

bubble. No one would see it, and no one would run into it. Its purpose was to block us from magical view. It was kind of like plopping a slice of another plane of existence in the middle of this one. The average person would never notice, even though there would be a slight shift in their perception and being when they walked through it, because people tended to only see what they wanted.

And because it wasn't part of this world, someone like Vidar couldn't reach out magically and find us. He wouldn't know we were here unless he was in the room with us.

Frey's club, NEON, had wards like this by default, which was why I was safe there. He and Dahlia put them in place. But out here, I had to use my ring's power, and give it an extra push with my own Valkyrie magic.

"What happened to Nico?" Bragi interrupted the silence between us.

"How...?" I left the question incomplete on purpose. Whatever Bragi chose to interpret in it could give me more answers than being direct.

He downed his coffee in a single swallow. "I felt when he died."

They were that close? No, that wasn't what Bragi said, and I wouldn't make assumptions. This would be a draining conversation if we were both testing each other's boundaries and I was fighting between attraction and revulsion.

"Nico came to find me after..." *I realized how many lies you'd told me, and I kicked you out of my life.* "After we walked away from you. He took me out for a picnic." *Fuck* that was a bittersweet memory. "Vidar found us, and Nico..." I drew in a shaky breath. Damn it, why did I have to let this get to me in front of anyone?

I steeled myself and pushed ice through my veins. "Nico exploded himself to distract Vidar long enough for me to get away." Because Nico was a phoenix. He'd just come back after. Neither of us was naive enough to believe he could destroy Vidar, who had done several things to himself to make him even harder to destroy than other immortals.

"That's what I felt." Bragi seemed to be talking to himself as much as me. "Nico's back now, though?"

I couldn't lie, because Bragi would feel it, and this was what I needed his help with. "Yes. But he doesn't remember who he is." Or who I was.

Bragi frowned. Was that fear whispering from him?

How would I feel that?

"It means this is his last life." Bragi's words landed hard. "Maybe it's fate's way of saying *thanks for playing; here, have a normal run,* but I think it's just cruel. I've never seen it happen before, but he told me that the other phoenixes, after they lost their memories... That was it. He didn't see them again. Once he's gone, there are no more phoenixes."

The entire notion made my stomach churn, and I pushed away my food. Nico wasn't the last, because one of the babies inside me was the next. I couldn't linger on that because who knew what Bragi would glean from those emotions?

I could focus on the grief, on the idea of losing Nico for good, though. Bragi could choke on those feelings for all I cared.

"We have to help him get his memories back." I didn't see any other answer.

"That's not how it works."

Bullshit. I'd heard that from the gods so many times over the years, and proved them wrong more often than not. "I lost my Valkyrie powers, and you helped me get them back."

My retort triggered new memories. Walking through a door in the bottom of a grandfather clock in Bragi's house, into a clearing in the fae realm. A tiny pocket of beauty. Spending hours—days—with him drawing his fingers over my bare skin.

Yeah, it hurt like hell. The way he explained it, he was breaking various ethereal connections inside me, and letting them re-heal—like having to break a bone that had knit together wrong, but thousands of times over.

"I had to torture you." Bragi's frown deepened. "And you hadn't lost your power, you were just cut off from it."

"That's probably the case with Nico, too. He

always has his memories when he's reborn, and he has the same fucking body. You're telling me whatever magic brings him back exactly like he was before decided to restore everything about him except his past?"

"You're telling me you don't think magic is that precise and unpredictable?"

I'd seen powers used for things more intricate than brain surgery, and there were many elements of it that couldn't be explained. Like, why did Dahlia seem like a regular mortal until she was in her early thirties and suddenly manifested as a full-on dragon?

"There's always a catch. A loophole. Something. Even if those memories are truly gone"—I hated the thought—"you can tell him what he needs to know. You can tell him about who he is."

"No. I can tell him who he *was*."

The desperation was sinking in and I couldn't stop it. I didn't know how Nico had managed to work his way into my heart so quickly, but I needed him in my life and I needed him to be whole.

"So I tell him who he is, and then what? The two of you live happily ever after?" Disdain oozed from Bragi's question.

"Maybe." Hopefully. I would never admit it out loud, and I hated that the thought existed in my head, but watching Dahlia with her men made me jealous. They adored her, they were good to her, and they shared a bond I never would've believed until I met them.

She was my BFF, my sister forever, and we'd do anything for each other. But that kind of love, what she had with Fen and Frey, was different. And it ached to see. Was it wrong to want something similar for myself?

"Okay," Bragi said.

I stared at him in disbelief. He'd given me what I wanted, but I didn't expect that. "Really? If I asked you to go with me right now to go see him, you'd do it? No conditions?"

"I do have something I want—"

I opened my mouth to say *you can't have me.*

"—but it's not a condition of helping you." Bragi talked over me. "If you want to go now, we can."

Fuck yes. I shoved the rest of the muffin in my mouth, washed it down with wonderfully sweet coffee, and said, "Let's go." I held out my hand and waited for him to blink us away.

Bragi shook his head. "You drive."

Whatever. I didn't know what his angle was, but I'd worry about it later. We were going to get Nico back.

CHAPTER 3

NICODEMUS

Every morning that I woke up in this house, it was a little more familiar.

Unlike a month ago when I opened my eyes to find myself in a bed I didn't recognize, in a house I swore I'd never seen before, and in a body that must be mine, but I couldn't give a name to. I'd had no idea where I was. Who I was.

My initial reaction should have been panic, and that was certainly there, but enough of my brain said *it's fine* that I was able to think my way through not freaking out.

I'd toured the house, which didn't take long. There was the room I'd woken up in, a small sitting area, and a bathroom with a stand-up shower. The kitchen wasn't large, but it was beautiful. Warm, clean, perfectly organized, and host to pans and utensils I couldn't name any more than I could name myself.

I would discover over the following weeks that my muscle memory knew how to use every single item I picked up in that room.

My home—I knew it was mine because the people who lived around me confirmed it—was decorated with stunning paintings and sculptures, vases and books, and not a single photograph or image of me with anyone else.

About a week after I woke up, I discovered a small watercolor painting, tucked into the drawer of a desk, that showed me in a frilled shirt, posing with a gorgeous man and a laughing redhead. The parchment looked like it might crumble if I held it too long, so I'd left it where I found it.

The wallet in a dish by my front door had an ID with a picture of me, that said my name was Nicodemus. The handful of credit and bank cards had the same name on them.

I talked to the neighbors. The people in town. They all recognized me, and called me *Nico*. When I tried to ask who I was, few had answers for me. Several of the merchants said I was always friendly. My neighbors said I waved whenever I walked by.

They all treated me with a level of deference and respect that felt overstated for someone living such an understated life, and they all said I tended to keep to myself.

I'd gone to the local clinic for my amnesia, and they sent me to a real hospital for a series of tests. Physically I was fine, according to every single doctor. *Your memory will probably come back with time,* they told me.

Not reassuring.

On top of that, while I didn't know who I was, I seemed to know that most people didn't believe in things like magic and shape shifters and that gods walked among us, but that it was all true. I had enough knowledge to recognize the reality and that I should keep it to myself.

Quite unhelpful in the grand scheme of things.

A few weeks ago, a stunning redhead approached me on the streets. She looked vaguely like the woman in the watercolor image, but my instinct said they weren't the same person.

Nico. The way she'd said my name sent shivers of pleasure racing over me, and the way she kissed me...

Incredible. I should've gotten more information from her. A phone number. An address.

Finding *Magnus* in the world wasn't as simple as it seemed, and I hadn't seen her in town since that first day.

I really wanted to. Every day when I went out, I hoped she would show up again. Give me another one of those kisses. Tell me who she was.

Who I was.

I wasn't surprised by the knock on my door—the

people around here stopped by on a regular basis with food, just to say *hi*.

Maybe I was a god—for some reason I had knowledge that people gave food offerings to gods, even though I had no idea what I'd been doing with my life two months ago—but if I were some sort of great and magical being, I didn't remember how to use any of my power.

When I saw *her*—the woman with the sad-but-kind face framed in flowing auburn curls—on my front step, desire spilled through me. She was prettier than I remembered. And looked sadder.

The man with her balanced my reaction with caution. His brown hair and the hint of a muscled build under his clothing was easy to look at, but something about him set off *Caution* bells in my mind. Especially because unlike her, he *was* the person from the painting.

How?

Another question I didn't have answers to.

"Can I help you?" I asked.

"We met the other day," Magnus said. "Again."

"I remember." Such a deceptive response.

The way her mouth twitched, the corners pulling down, made me think she agreed. "I ran off without giving you more information. I wasn't thinking clearly, I was hurt, and the situation is... complicated."

"I'm glad you're back. Would you like to come in?

Can you tell me who I am?" I stepped aside and opened the door wider. Was I setting myself up for disappointment to hope these two could unravel my broken mind the way no one else had been able to?

She almost smiled. I wanted the full experience, like that first time she approached me. How could I get that joy back?

"Yes, to both," she said. "Rather, I can tell you a little. I didn't know you for long, but I feel like I learned a lot about you. He, on the other hand..." She jerked her head at her companion. "He can tell you *a lot.*"

"Bragi." He extended his hand, and I shook it. "We've known each other off and on for centuries."

Interesting. Warmth and a spark of familiarity danced along my skin at his touch, but it didn't erase my trepidation.

They stepped inside, and Bragi seemed to know exactly where he was going. Not that it was a complicated layout in here, but there was no hesitation as he turned toward the living room and made himself comfortable on the couch.

"Make yourself at home," Magnus muttered. She lingered near the edge of the room, arms crossed and gaze darting in every direction.

Bragi shrugged and leaned back into the cushions. "I did."

They came here together, but it didn't take an empath to detect the animosity between them. I paused next to Magnus and pointed her toward the room. "You can have a seat."

"I'm a little wound up." She sounded apologetic. "Thank you, though."

"How about some tea? I think I have some scones. Or coffee?" I was fumbling. It seemed important that I leave a good impression.

They both assured me they were fine.

Okay, then. What I wanted to do was dump every question that had crossed my mind since I woke up without memories. That didn't seem like an effective approach, though. I settled on, "How do we know each other, Magnus?"

There was that almost-smile again. "You saved my life. Twice. In between, we were getting close."

"I saved *your* life?" Why did that surprise me? Was I heroic? Was she a goddess? A goddess probably wouldn't need saving, but she was that level of awe-inspiring.

She nodded. "You did save me. Yes."

"Who are you?" I needed to know from both of them. "Not your names, but... What do you do?" As in, their work? I didn't have the right words to ask what I truly meant.

Neither of them looked fazed by the question, though.

"I'm a Valkyrie," Magnus said as if it were the most casual thing ever. "And Bragi's a professional asshole."

"I prefer the term *bard*, though historically there are a lot of similarities." He didn't look bothered by her description. "For these purposes, I'm a god of art and music." Did he falter? Was that untrue?

"Do you remember what you are? How much do you know?" Magnus asked.

Nothing. I had so little information about me, I couldn't even answer the demographic information when someone had come door to door with a political survey. "I have impressions. Instincts. I know how to interact with the world around me. But when it comes to *me*? I don't remember any details about me or if I know anyone else."

I'd explained a variation on that so many times recently, to doctors and neighbors and the local priest, but repeating now filled me with a new kind of despair.

"Do you want to show him, Magnus?" Bragi asked. "See if it jogs something?"

She furrowed her brow and studied him. "Why me?"

"You're stunningly impressive and impossible to ignore in full regalia."

At Bragi's words, images flashed in my mind. As much impression as solid visual. Wings—auburn like her hair. Flame. Feathers.

Magnus took a few steps away from me, toward the center of the room where there was more space. In a blink, her jeans and NEON T-shirt were gone, replaced with the most intricate and impractical armor in existence. Chain mail that hugged her torso and ended in a short skirt. Skull pauldrons. Leather leggings, covered by shin guards leading to boots.

And full, deep red wings folded against her back.

"*Wow*." I didn't try to stop the exclamation from slipping out. "You were beautiful before, but this... *Wow*."

The blush that dotted her cheeks was pretty and out of place on the warrior who stood in front of me. "What do a god and a Valkyrie want with me?" What was I to them?

Someone she felt comfortable playing tonsil tag with, in the middle of a small town.

I saved her life. How?

"You're the last of your kind," Bragi said.

Magnus's armor vanished, and her street clothes were back. "A phoenix."

What? No. "As in, death and rebirth? Rising from the ashes?"

"Yes. As in a few weeks ago, you and I were out and we were attacked by a god." As she spoke, Magnus's voice went hard.

This couldn't be real. Of all the scenarios I'd put myself in, while I struggled with not knowing me, this never made the list. A phoenix? And a *god* attacked me? I turned to Bragi. "Was it you?"

They both scowled, though I felt like it was for different reasons.

"No," Magnus said. "This one is named Vidar."

The word sent an unpleasant shiver up my spine. "Is that why I don't remember anything?" A fucking *phoenix*?

"Yes. You and I were on a date." Magnus seemed to be riding an emotional roller coaster, and watching her ups and downs was almost as dizzying as being on an actual ride. "You exploded him, and in the process... exploded yourself."

But I wasn't dead now. Because I was a phoenix. The most disconcerting thing about her story was that part of me believed it without question. Like when I'd woken up without my memories and wanted to panic. This was the same voice that said I didn't need to. "Did I kill him?"

"No. But you bought me time to get away. And now you've returned."

I held my arms out in front of me and turned them over again and again. "I'm not like a baby bird or anything—I'm a full-grown man."

Bragi leaned forward in his seat, the casual demeanor fading. "You told me once that coming back as a baby each time was counterintuitive, so each time you were reborn, you picked up where you left off. With your body, your memories..."

That was convenient. "Except I don't have my memories. There's a plot hole in your tale."

"My stories do *not* have plot holes." An edge

crept into Bragi's voice. "They have elements the reader doesn't understand."

"This is a lot to absorb." So much that I struggled to wrap my brain around it. Recognizing that magic was real, musing for fun about being a god, was a far cry from a stunning woman and a man from a painting in a drawer showing up and saying *you're literally one of a kind.*

I wanted to keep asking questions. I wanted *all* the information about me. However, if they shared everything at once, my mind might rupture with disbelief. "How do you two know each other?" I needed to redirect the topic while my mind chewed on this information about me.

They exchanged looks, and Magnus shrugged. "You're the storyteller, Bragi."

"Where to start?" He let out a long breath.

Magnus finally sank into a nearby chair. "At the beginning. Don't leave things out just because they paint you in a bad light."

"It is what it is." Bragi didn't sound as casual as the words implied. "This story works best with some background information. I'll try not to have us here all afternoon."

They could keep me here all year if it meant their company over my own fractured mind. "Take whatever time you need."

"A long, long time ago—"

"Not like a couple hundred years, like before the dinosaurs." Magnus cut Bragi off.

He glared at her. "You wanted me to tell this."

She made a show of clamping her mouth shut.

"I didn't expect you to start at the beginning of time." I chuckled as much to keep the mood light as anything.

"Not that long ago," Bragi said. "But closer to then, than to now. Back then, a trio of dragons— sisters—wrote a series of prophecies. They didn't call them that. The three thought they were just telling each other stories."

"Until humanity came along, and those stories started coming true," Magnus added.

Bragi gave her another pointed stare, and she huffed.

The two of them clashed, but it wasn't like oil and water, it was like air and fire. One met the other and combusted. It was terrifying and alluring and comfortable.

"For the sake of Magnus's millennial attention span—"

"Fuck you, old man." She stuck her tongue out at him.

He smirked. "Too easy."

She scowled.

There was no way the two of them weren't fucking.

"The prophecies." Bragi spoke in an *anyway* sort

of tone. "They involve things like the end-ish of the world. As in, for most people, it seems like the world has ended, but since it's already happened multiple times, obviously life goes on. One of those times is coming up, and involves a lot of gods."

"Like you?" I asked.

"Yes. Like me. Many of us will be replaced or killed or simply lose our power. All things gods don't care for."

"I can't imagine most care for those things." I certainly didn't like finding out I was a once-powerful being who didn't remember any of my legacy, and was on my last leg, so to speak.

"And now we have a sympathetic protagonist." Bragi sounded smug.

Magnus wasn't impressed. "He didn't say that."

"These gods formed a coalition." Bragi kept talking as if she hadn't said anything. "A board, if you will. And..." His bravado faltered, and he clenched his jaw.

Curious.

Magnus let out a long exhale. "And they adopted a bunch of little orphan mortals who had the potential to become powerful beings ourselves, and trained us as their own little army, complete with soldiers, and assassins who would kill anyone those gods considered a threat."

"That's horrible." I wouldn't even want to see that in a story, but they were talking about real life.

"It is," Bragi said. "And in case you haven't guessed, I was one of those gods and Magnus was one of those assassins."

"But you're a Valkyrie," I said to her.

"I had the potential to become more. So I did." She almost made it sound like a motivational poster.

One with what I suspected was an immense amount of trauma behind its creation.

"Some of the gods have met their fate already." Bragi picked up the story again. "Another of those gods, Vidar, is very much still alive and powerful. He tried to destroy Magnus and her best friend"—

Magus cleared her throat loudly.

—"Sister," Bragi said, "and he failed. They lived. So he tricked each of them into thinking the other was dead."

Magnus visibly shuddered, and I wanted to reach out and comfort her. Wrap her up and protect her. I doubted she needed any sort of savior most of the time, but the impulse was there regardless.

Instead, I settled for resting a hand on her shoulder.

She gave me a glance and an almost-smile.

"When that happened, Magnus came to me. She was hurt, so very badly." It sounded like it caused Bragi pain to say those words. "Your tears helped bring her back to life, and I helped rehabilitate her."

"He's leaving out the best part." Bitterness dripped from Magnus's voice. "He let me continue to think Dahlia was dead, though he knew better, and kept you and me imprisoned in his home in the process."

"I kept Vidar from killing you and I'd do it again without hesitation."

I felt like I understood more now than I had in the last month. Not much about me, but certainly about the people whose company I kept. "Was I in on the deception?"

"No." They answered me in unison.

Which meant at some point, we must have left Bragi's protection, or he let us go. I suspected I'd get two different answers if I asked which it was. "How old am I?"

"Thousands of years. Older than me and beyond that, I don't know," Bragi said.

Holy fuck.

Magnus tensed under my grip. "Something's wrong."

There was another knock as she spoke.

"I'll be right back." I pulled away.

She grabbed my wrist, and worked her jaw up and down, then gave a rapid shake of her head. "Be careful."

Answering my door? That didn't bode well.

When I opened the front door, I found myself face to face with a man in what I assumed was an expensive suit. His hair was slicked back, and there wasn't a single wrinkle in his pinstripes. He greeted me with a warm smile that sent waves of cold through me.

"Afternoon," he said, and looked past me. "Hello, Lover."

Terror and rage bled into my thoughts. Who was this man?

"Vidar." Magnus's voice came from behind me.

The killing god?

Fuck.

CHAPTER 4

MAGNUS

Fury coiled with nausea, winding me tight until I was ready to snap from the tension.

How did Vidar find us?

I had protections in place to hide us from magical view. From anyone looking for us. Bragi should be doing the same. We should not only be invisible to magical beings, we should be double invisible.

Unless Bragi took my shields down instead of putting his own up?

All those thoughts passed through my mind in the blink that it took me to summon my full Valkyrie armor again, along with a physical shield and weapon.

I stalked toward Vidar, brushing past the others as he said *Hello, Lover*.

I wouldn't lose Nico again, and I definitely

wasn't letting anyone know about or hurt my children. I wouldn't lose anyone to Vidar again.

Wrapping Vidar and myself in a compact bubble, I blinked us to a spot in the middle of the Australian outback with nothing but tumbleweeds and rocks for miles.

I'd be pleased about the look of shock on his face if I wasn't about to vomit over the fact that he was so nearby. I settled for lunging at him, sword drawn and pointed at his throat. If I couldn't kill him, maybe I could catch him off-guard enough to do serious damage, so I could flee and make a real plan.

My blade stopped, seemingly with the tip pressed to his jugular, and refused to penetrate his skin.

Vidar raised his brows and stared at me, having recovered from whatever surprise would give me an advantage. "Let's not do that," he said.

He must have an invisible shield in place as well. The magical version of paper-thin bulletproof glass.

I wore one too, and I shifted it to wrap around both of us, tightening the sphere around him and using my might to press in. If I couldn't cut him, I'd squash him.

But my forcefield struck his and refused to budge.

It didn't matter. As long as he was standing in front of me, watching me with amusement and curiosity, I could keep trying. I poured all my strength into the sword, and focused my power on the tip of the blade as well, pushing to crack through a single point in his defenses.

"Why aren't you fighting back?" I forced the question through gritted teeth.

Vidar remained cool. Infuriatingly so. "That's not why I'm here."

"Your mistake." I strained and pushed harder. I was making progress. The sword was penetrating, but it was slow. Like watching grass grow or paint dry or Qui Gon cut through a steel door with his lightsaber.

Vidar clucked, but didn't otherwise move. "It was never about killing you. Do you realize that yet?"

He was telling the truth. The reality wafted toward me on unsettling waves.

Yeah. Okay. More like I was letting him distract me. "Then why are you working so hard to step in my path at every turn?" I shouldn't engage with him, but I was determined to cut him, and what else was I going to do in the meantime? Wordle?

"I'll make you the same offer I made Bragi. Back off, let me have Dahlia, and I'll leave you alone. I'll stop hunting you. You can go back to your life. She's my target."

That wasn't completely true. This time I felt a hint of deception.

Or I knew it was there, because his mouth was moving.

"Are you fucking serious? I'd do anything for Dahlia." I'd walked away from her once. Taken Vidar's side when I still believed he was in the right. I could never make up for that mistake, but I didn't abandon the people I loved. The people who would do the same for me in return.

"Which is why you keep getting caught up in this," Vidar said. "She's the threat. You're just irritating."

I pushed harder on my blade. Focused more into narrowing my shield into a point to slip through the cracks in his and split it. "You know my answer. Why the fuck are you asking?"

Despite the fact that the sun beat down on us, and hot wind whipped around us, the way he smiled sent ice spilling through my veins.

"I can sense magical energy. I can tell when it's attached to individuals. Gods. Immortals. Potentials."

"Big fucking deal." I knew that already. Dahlia could do a version of the same, but hers could integrate with technology. Why did Vidar think it was important to bring that up now?

"I can sense that you and I aren't the only ones here," he said.

No.

His smirk twisted further. Into something darker. "Two more. Overlapped with you. Wouldn't you like them to survive long enough that you can raise them?"

"*Don't touch them.*" I pushed every ounce of power I could find, reaching past my limits, to force my blade into him. The only headway I made was shouting in agony, but I kept trying.

"Walk away from Dahlia."

No. Never. "I will burn you down." I bit off the words. "I don't know how, but somehow, before you hurt me or my family, I will obliterate everything you ever were. I swear it here and now, on what will be your ashes."

"She's not even your real sis—"

I wrapped him in a bubble of pocket reality, sealed it tight, and sent him to the bottom of the Mariana Trench.

It wouldn't take him long to break free. An hour at the outside, but more likely minutes. Until then, he wouldn't be able to sense anything but himself and the suffocating pressure.

Like he'd subjected us to in school.

I blinked myself back to Nico's, grasping at a million strands of thought, to figure out which got my attention first.

Nico and Bragi had returned to the living room, and Nico stared at me with wide eyes, the instant I appeared in front of them.

"Seeing it is different than knowing it's real." Awe filled his voice.

I wanted to bask in the adoration, but there

wasn't time. First things first, I doubled down on the protective wards that should hide us from everyone, including Vidar.

Then I stalked toward Bragi, sword still drawn, and faced him down the same way I had Vidar.

This time though, I broke the skin. "You exposed us." I growled. "You yanked down my wards, and you let Vidar find us." I never should've talked to him, let alone brought him here. I was an idiot.

"I swear to you, I didn't." The fear that flashed in Bragi's eyes was tangible.

I could taste it. "How am I supposed to trust anything you say? Ever?" Besides the fact that I felt the truth radiating from him, the way I had with Vidar when he told me he didn't want to kill me.

A drop of blood welled from Bragi's throat, at the tip of my blade.

"You're right. I am still lying to you." His tone smoothed again. Was that... *Relief?*

How was I feeling all of this?

Unless I was imagining what I wanted to be there.

No. Because if Bragi was still lying to me, after everything we'd been through, after all his insistence that it was all for me... I gripped my weapon harder. "Lying about what?"

"I couldn't have broken your spells because I don't have any power."

I pressed the sword to him, making another drop

of blood well up and vanish in an instant under a healed wound. "You look fine to me."

"I can still heal. But I can't do anything else." He spoke through gritted teeth.

"Could we not... Not in here?" Nico pleaded.

I hated to leave a bad impression on him, but some things were more important than appearances. Him not wanting Bragi to bleed on his rugs was reasonable, though.

I focused on Bragi. "Prove it."

"You can't prove the absence of a thing," Bragi said.

Nico stepped up next to him. "You really can't. That's like asking someone to prove their package never arrived. Please don't torture him."

I put on a strong front, talked a big game, all that. I'd been raised as a killer, and not flinching at the sight of suffering came with that.

But I didn't like any of that, and as furious as I was with Bragi for *everything*, I didn't want to stand here and slice little bits off him to prove any sort of anything. There was one thing I could do. If he was telling the truth it didn't matter, and if he was lying about being powerless... This one served him right.

I took the leash off of my hate and my fear. I let all of my doubt and desperation flow free. Every single negative thought that I usually spent energy containing slammed into my mind, open for the world to see.

For Bragi to feel.

I gasped at the internal onslaught. Tears pricked my eyelids and a fist clenched around my chest, choking off my breath.

But Bragi didn't so much as bat an eye.

Though, the longer he and Nico watched me, the more their brows both furrowed.

"Are you all right?" Nico reached for me as I squeezed my eyes shut.

Bragi must've too, because I felt two hands grasp my bare arms.

And the concern rushed in. The confusion. Neither one mine, but both potent and heavy. The affection. The adoration.

The obsession.

The external wave blanketed my own feelings and wrapped my mind up in an awkward bandage of comfort. Someone felt those things. About me.

Summoning immense strength, I tucked it all aside again. Shoved everything that was mine into the closet in the back of my mind. Turned out that *never feel unless it's convenient* training they gave us in school was good for something.

I would break later. In private.

I focused on Bragi again, who looked worried, but not any shade of pained. "Nothing?" I asked.

He shrugged. "About what?"

Unless he'd learned a new trick in the last month

or so, he was telling the truth. His empathy, and likely most of his god powers, were gone.

From what he'd told me, once upon a time, he felt the intense emotions from others so strongly it was like being cut or breaking a bone. Being stabbed through the heart. He could teach himself to enjoy the pain, in a sadistic sort of way, but he still felt it.

"So the wards I have protecting us... failed?" I needed to focus on the problem at hand, and stay out of my own heart and past. "No. That's never happened before."

Bragi quirked his mouth in barely-suppressed amusement. Yeah, he wasn't impacted by the fucked-up state of my mind. "The number of times I've heard that..."

"Sometimes magic doesn't work, correct?" Nico was more sympathetic. "Like any skill, it's not always perfect?"

"It doesn't typically fail without the wielder knowing. Unless something is interfering." Did that mean we were still exposed? I thought I was hiding us from Vidar, and I wasn't? I pushed more power into the shield that severed us from the human plane.

Bragi's expression shifted to concern. "Have you taken up drinking strange teas? Nightshade perhaps? Or wearing crystals?" He trailed his gaze over me.

Nico tilted his head. There was that curiosity

again. "I feel like I should know this. What would interfere?"

"Countless things," Bragi said. "Other magic. The bearer being weak—"

"I'm not weak." I bit off the words and fixed him with a narrow-eyed glare.

He shook his head. "No. You're not."

Then what was doing this to me?

CHAPTER 5
BRAGI

I was sitting in a house with one immortal who had no idea who he was and what he could do, another who didn't know if her magic was working, and there was me. I was definitely a liability.

On top of that, the prophecies said both of them were doomed, because I loved them. Talk about a shitty situation.

I never should've brought Magnus here. I wanted to warn her. Make sure she and Nico were okay.

But more, I wanted to see them. I wouldn't let my selfishness destroy them. "If you don't have magic shielding you from view, you need to take Nico, and go back to NEON."

Magnus clenched her jaw, looking like she was ready to argue.

Or maybe she was just thinking about slapping me on principle. I hated not being able to feel—

I would not think that thought, because my mind was so much quieter, my mind more stable, without the onslaught of other's emotions every second of every fucking day.

"He's right," Nico said. "If being here is putting you in danger, you need to go where you're safe."

Magnus pinched the bridge of her nose. "Thanks for the advice, boys. You know I'm ten times the fighter either of you are, especially now."

"And Vidar still kicks your ass every time." I hated to phrase it that way, but if she was being stubborn, I would push her buttons.

She met my gaze with a hard glare, and never looked away while she grabbed her phone and dialed. "I need your help," she said into the device after a few seconds.

Did my provocation actually work?

Dahlia appeared in the middle of the room, looking nothing like the dragon she was. She wore denim shorts that ended in tulle, like a tutu, over glittery purple tights. Her shirt had drums that said *Plaid Peanut Butter* on the bass drum face, and her hair was flecked with purple glitter.

I bet her aunts hated that, which amused me.

She and Magnus weren't biological sisters, but growing up the way they did, living the life TOM had put them through, had driven them closer than any blood relatives.

"You're just hanging out in the open." Dahlia sounded concerned.

Magnus made a noise that was half-huff, half-growl. "I don't mean to be. Apparently I don't have full control over... something."

Dahlia snapped her fingers. "All fixed." She looked at Nico. "That should keep anyone from finding you."

"Vidar already has." Magnus's voice went tiny.

He had, and yet she walked away unscathed. What impossible decision did he offer her in exchange for her life? I'd worked with the man for centuries, and only severed ties recently. I knew how he thought. She was only here because it served him.

Fuck, I needed a way to keep her safe.

"I'm sorry. Have we met?" Nico asked.

Dahlia gave him an almost-smile. "Only twice. I'm Dahlia. Magnus's sister." She extended her hand.

He shook it. "Nico. But you already know that."

"I did. It's a pleasure to meet you again, regardless."

"It's not safe for them here." I wasn't surprised when Dahlia fixed me with a glare. I didn't give a fuck, as long as she helped protect Nico and Magnus, since I couldn't.

"I suppose you want to take them back to your place again? Put up a magical wall so no one including me can see them? So you can keep them *safe* and all to yourself?" Derision and disbelief dripped from Dahlia's every word.

Before I could provide a sharp retort, Magnus said, "He can't. He lost his power."

Dahlia snorted. "Okay." Her laugh was clipped. "Nico should be fine here, and Magnus, you come back to NEON with me, so Vidar doesn't find you."

"He already has." I repeated in hard words and grabbed Dahlia's wrist, to hold her attention. "You need to hide them, away from here and away from you."

A hissing sound slid from deep in Dahlia's throat and she fixed me with a rage-filled gaze. Heat tickled my palm. "You don't get a say in this. You're lucky she even talked to you." As Dahlia spoke, my hand grew warmer. Uncomfortably so.

"I want the same thing you do." I wouldn't pull away, even as the areas where my flesh met hers heated to scalding. My skin would blister any second now. "For the people I love to be safe."

"You don't love Magnus; you're obsessed with her. How the fuck do you not know the difference?"

My hand was an unhealthy shade of red, and my skin was cracking. I'd moved past second degree burns. "You and your gods would burn the world to the ground for each other. You're going to tell me that's not obsession? Put Magnus and Nico somewhere else, and walk away from her. For her. For you."

"I'll never abandon her," Dahlia said.

The muscles in my hand no longer worked. My palm was black and the skin was falling away. I let go of her with a grunt, and bit the inside of my cheek to keep from screaming as the skin grew back in a blink.

"Both men need to go with me. Somewhere that's not NEON." Magnus could've said that sooner. "Bragi is the only one we know who might have answers."

For Nico. That was the unspoken second half of her thought.

"Besides," Nico said. "From what you've told me and what I've seen so far, this Vidar person would be quite unhappy to have Bragi vanish from his sight."

That was true. He'd known where I was for the last month and hadn't come after me, but I didn't think for a moment that I'd fallen off his radar.

Dahlia's nostrils flared and she looked like she was struggling with an internal conflict. "We can't trust him."

"You can trust him to do one thing—not tell anyone where we are," Magnus said.

"I have a place—"

"No." Dahlia cut me off. "You don't get to pick where they hide."

Willful, irritating... But that was part of what had drawn me to Magnus. "You have a better idea?"

"I have a place." Magnus dragged the words out, as if she were reluctant to admit it.

My shock was mirrored on Dahlia's face. "You do?" She asked.

"It's not much. It's tiny. It's in the middle of nowhere in Wyoming. I picked it up after we decided to leave TOM, but before everything with Hel dying, and Vidar... It's not in my name. It was always meant to be a last resort."

Which we were reaching, apparently.

Dahlia frowned. "You never told me."

"Safer if no one knows, right?" Magnus looked apologetic.

If not even Dahlia knew of the place's existence, it would make it harder for Vidar to track us down.

Dahlia's expression didn't ease. "Yeah. I can know now, right? So I can take us there and set up wards?"

"I'll take us," Magnus said. "You'll know anyway once we're there. It's not so easy to say *little hut in the middle of nowhere* and have it mean anything. Nico, I'm sorry to have dragged you into this. I just want you to remember who you are."

"I want that too." There was only kindness in his reply. "From what you've said—what I've seen—about this Vidar, he may not have let me have peace regardless. If this gets me answers, I'd like to go with you."

Reasonable to a fault, except when he was pushed. There was the man I remembered loving.

"It'll be like going on holiday. My first. I'll go pack." Nico headed into his bedroom.

He emerged a few minutes later with a suitcase that looked like it had been purchased in the fifties —the 1850's—and set it on the ground at his feet. "I'm ready."

Magnus looked at me and I nodded a confirmation.

Dahlia grasped one of her hands, and Nico took the other and mine. In a blink, we were in a sparsely decorated living room, with wooden walls, a small kitchen, and a stairway leading up to a bedroom loft, that looked out over it all.

"It's cozy." I would spend more time looking around, but that took mere seconds.

Magnus fixed me with a glare. "It was meant for just me."

Dahlia twisted her mouth. "Wards are up. They're not as complicated as the ones around NEON, but the cabin exists in a different plane now, and I'll know if anyone else walks inside the circle." The trademark cheer was gone from her voice.

"Thank you. You should go," Magnus said.

The lines on Dahlia's forehead creased deeper. "Do you want food? Supplies?"

"Oh. Yeah," Magnus said.

This was awkward.

Magnus gave a hard shake of her head, and I practically heard the thoughts slotting into place. "Now that you know where this is, Dahlia, will you grab food, and my clothes?" That made sense, because Dahlia could blink in and out of NEON and the connected buildings, where most couldn't magically pass those wards. "I'll take Bragi and Nico—"

"No." Dahlia cut her off. "He doesn't get to be alone with you."

By *he* she meant *me* and it was a ridiculous stand to take, given she was about to leave me here with Magnus long term. I would make this concession, if it meant Dahlia gave us some peace. "I'll go with Dahlia. I already have a suitcase in Chicago, and I need to check out of my hotel."

"Why do you have a hot...?" Dahlia trailed off with a smirk. "No powers. You had to take a plane."

I was glad she found that amusing. *Not.*

Magnus took Nico's hand. "I'm sorry to keep bouncing you back and forth. We'll go grocery shopping. Make sure we're set for food for a little while."

"All right." Nico was taking this far better than most would in the same position.

"And tomorrow we'll go see Kirby, about memories and reincarnation," Dahlia said.

The way Magnus ducked her head, the shuffle of her feet, was too obvious. Too uncomfortable. I'd taught her better than that. "I can take care of all that. Bring Nico to her. You have other things to do."

A scowl flicked over Dahlia's face and then vanished. "I don't mind. I always like seeing the Rescue Rangers."

"Really, you don't need to go with us." All Magnus had to say was *I don't want you here, because Vidar threatened you*, but she wouldn't. Because then Dahlia would double down.

I wanted to step in, mediate, tell them both to knock it off. But Dahlia being here made things difficult, and she was unlikely to listen to me regardless.

"Okay." Dahlia gave Magnus a tight hug. "See you back here soon?"

Magnus nodded.

Dahlia squeezed my hand far more tightly than she needed to. "Where are you staying?"

I gave her the hotel name and the room number, and a dark cloud spread through the room. "That's a block from NEON."

"You're surprised?" I asked.

Dahlia growled and dug claws into my palm. In a blink, we were in my hotel room.

"I'll be in the lobby in fifteen minutes. Be there, or I leave you." Dahlia vanished before I could reply.

She wouldn't leave me, because Magnus needed my help.

As I did what little packing was required, I stalled on a short stack of notebooks. They were journals—mine—from more than a century ago. I'd almost forgotten I brought them, and when I originally packed them, I wasn't sure why.

This stack was from the decades where I met Nico. Where we were together. They were more an insight into my raw thoughts than any sort of story, but they might jar memories loose that I'd pushed aside.

Which was both a good and a bad reason for me to read them. I may pull them out again, but I wasn't certain. Still, they were coming with me.

I finished packing, and I was waiting for Dahlia when she returned.

We blinked back to the cabin to find Magnus and Nico in the kitchen, putting away groceries. That almost looked domestic. The sight of them working side-by-side ached with familiarity. Nico wouldn't be happy working in that tiny space, but he loved to cook and he'd make it work. I already knew.

Dahlia handed Magnus a suitcase.

"I'll feel if anyone breaches the wards," Dahlia said. "Be safe."

Magnus gave her another tight hug. "I promise. I'll talk to you soon."

Dahlia stepped away, and the way she tapped her fingers against her leg radiated hesitation. I knew it without being able to feel it. Then she vanished from the room.

Magnus breathed the tiniest sigh of relief when

Dahlia left. I could guess what Vidar offered her, but I wasn't going to voice the thought. He'd told her she had to pick between Dahlia and something else. Nico, maybe? Magnus thought she could do both.

I couldn't steal that hope from her, and it wouldn't hurt her to not tell her that she was wrong.

"So, uh…" Nico's words and noisy exhale shattered the silence but not the lingering discomfort. "I don't feel as though I like being the center of attention, but given the circumstances, I don't suppose this is a good time to ask you to tell me more about me."

Ambivalence trickled in my veins. Telling stories about *before* was one of my favorite past times, but there was a whole lot of bittersweetness attached to the Nico memories.

That was why I was here, though—at least part of the reason—and I could deliver. "Anything specific you'd like to know?"

"I'm not so interested in statistics." Nico nudged Magnus from the kitchen and toward the living room. "Dates and numbers are all well and good, but they don't say much about a person. I want to hear about who I knew. Were you and I close, Bragi?"

"Once upon a time." As all good stories started. Or in our case, ended. "We were lovers." Though I knew nothing would be there, a part of me expected waves of emotion to go with Nico's curious expression and Magnus's scowl. Was this similar to the phantom pains an amputee felt?

Nico sat on the futon in the middle of the room, and Magnus only hesitated for a moment before taking the spot next to him.

That left one of the beanbags on the floor for me. I'd stand. That made the storytelling more epic anyway.

"I found a painting," Nico said. "Of me and you, Bragi. And a woman. It looked old."

Magnus's eyebrows rose almost to her hairline. "I'd like to hear *that* story."

I had zero interest in telling it. The ache it summoned made me want to box the memory up again.

"There's no story to tell. She didn't exist. I painted her—us—because I thought it would look pretty." That wasn't the full story. Nico and I had shared a vision of her long ago. The same woman. Someone we thought at the time couldn't exist, because we'd each dreamed of a Valkyrie and there weren't any left. Magnus wouldn't care for those details, so glossing over things was best.

"What about the rest of your past together?" Magnus looked suspicious, as if she didn't believe me.

Thankfully she didn't push for more. "Nico and I fell for each other over the course of decades. He kept his distance because a phoenix loses so many in their lifetime, and I was terrified of the way I was drawn to him."

Despite being long ago, the past flowed back easily once I nudged the edges. "I stumbled into this pub in Australia and they had the most incredible food."

"What were you doing in Australia?" Magnus looked at Nico, not me, when she asked the question.

Nico shrugged, and an almost-smile played on his face. "Eating?"

"Cooking," I said. "He'd decided to stretch his wings, so to speak, and that was where the trip took him. Nico used to do that—move from place to place every few decades, exchange work—mostly cooking—for room and board. I wanted to meet the man behind the meal, and once he and I started talking, we didn't want to stop."

It ached to remember how easy that first conversation had been. I couldn't recall most of the details, but I remembered how he felt and how I felt. "I hadn't had that kind of fun, that kind of connection in..." Ever? Not before them. "I was reluctant to leave at the end of the night."

"So you stayed?" Magnus asked.

There were many times I wished I had. "What kind of story would that be? I was, of course, the idiot who walked away rather than admit I wanted to do exactly the opposite. I spent a few years popping around the world, and found myself at a party in France." I loved parties. Performing. All those eyes on me. The adoration. It was my favorite kind of worship.

"I was the main event, quite unintentionally. I'd been invited by a friend of a friend, and one thing led to another until most of the house was gathered around, listening and laughing." That was the kind of emotion I could thrive on. At least back then. When did I lose that joy? "Then Nico walked in with another guest, and the only attention I wanted was his."

Nico gave a faint chuckle. "You were commanding an entire room. There's no way I was that fascinating."

"Oh, but you were. Not only because I'd stuffed myself on their adoration before you arrived." I winked. "But because everyone else in the room paled in comparison to remembering that one night I'd spent talking to you, a few years earlier." I glanced at Magnus. "There was the same kind of draw with you, but for different reasons."

"I have nicer tits." Sarcasm lined her retort, but so did amusement. "Besides, this isn't about me, it's about Nico."

I wanted to correct her—my attraction to Magnus had never been physical, though without question, she was stunning. Her mood was almost playful, and I didn't want to lose that.

"What happened next?" Nico was leaned in, eyes wide and fascination on his face.

He'd always been genuine. Sincere. Had a love of the simple things that made life incredible. Seeing it now made remembering then that much more potent.

"We walked away from the party," I said. "Down to a nearby lake. We spent the night talking. Making out under the stars."

"That sounds nice." Nico's smile grew.

Magnus didn't look so impressed. "It is. Is that a go to move for you, Bragi?"

"You two...?" Nico pointed between us.

"Not quite. Rather, yes, we've been together. And yes, there was a lake, and kissing." I adored the memory as much as I did the one of those first kisses with Nico. Thinking about the early days with him or Magnus awakened my senses and sent desire for times passed spilling through me. "But no other moment compares to either of those, with either of you."

Magnus raised her brows. "Yeah."

"It's true. You both see the world through different lenses, and there's no comparison. Nico is fascination and discovery and joy. Magnus, you're light in the shadows, and you refuse to be dimmed."

Her disbelief melted into a scowl, and then vanished behind a smile that was warm, genuine, and completely out of place. "Is anyone else hungry?" It was as if she'd flipped a switch, and shot off the melancholy and any emotion connected to the conversation.

Which meant regardless of what I said next, she'd be more focused on pretending to be a blank slate than on participating.

If I could still sense feeling, I knew hers wouldn't match her demeanor. Fuck that fucking school for teaching her to so effectively hide what was actually going on in her head.

And fuck me for having been a part of it.

CHAPTER 6
NICODEMUS

It was clear Magnus never meant to share this place with another individual, not long term, based on the full sized bed in the loft and the fact that the only other *bed* in the place was a futon couch that folded down to sleep on.

What kind of life did she come from where she had to decide in a blink whether or not to attack the person at the door, and hiding from the entire world was status quo?

Then there was Bragi... There was what he'd told me about why they were allies but didn't like each other, but I suspected there was a lot more to the story than I understood.

I was having as hard a time wrapping my mind around all of it as I was the news that I was a phoenix. How had I lived *any* of this, let alone *all* of it?

There was so much for me to absorb, and as far as I could tell, all this new information was based on the last thirty days of my life. If I was older than history, how had I remembered even a tenth of that up to this point?

As the night wound down, Bragi and I insisted Magnus take the bed. If anyone was going to share, it made sense she not be forced to sleep next to a man who didn't remember her or one who refused to let her forget him.

It was odd sleeping next to Bragi. The kind of familiar one felt walking into a room they didn't recognize, but they swore they'd been there before.

Breakfast in the morning was a stilted, awkward affair. Enough words were exchanged to accomplish not running into each other as we made coffee and ate cold cereal.

This was going to be a grand celebration of ongoing awkwardness. I hoped Magnus's friends could help me. I refused to remain a liability to her or Bragi.

We wrapped up and Magnus took us to our next destination to meet *Kirby*. Apparently this woman was a Valkyrie—the last before she realized the power to make more, like Magnus—and she'd lived multiple lives and dealt with missing memories too. When Magnus called her, Kirby didn't have any immediate insight to offer, but invited us over anyway, to see if she could figure something out.

Magnus landed us in front of a beautiful old cottage that looked like it could sit at the edge of the village I lived in. The entire feeling here was warmth and acceptance, but with a thread of *look away, there's nothing to see here* layered through it.

Interesting sensation. At the edge of the property, every time I tried to view the house directly, my gaze wandered somewhere else.

As we walked up the path, I found it easier to focus on the home. At the front door, there was an arrangement of symbols around the door. Not a single language, and none of them anything I recognized.

Or did I? Norse runes. Celtic words. Egyptian symbols. Who were these people?

Who was I?

Bragi stood half a step behind us, and Magnus knocked.

The woman who answered was attractive, with her blond hair pulled into a mid-ponytail, and strands wisping loose around her face. She was only a few inches shorter than Magnus, but the way she held herself, the invisible power she radiated, made her feel larger than life.

"Hey." The woman gave Magnus a tight smile and they exchanged hugs. "Why did you bring him?"

Magnus glanced over her shoulder at Bragi. "I keep asking myself the same thing, but I have reasons."

"Lovely to see you too, Kirby." Bragi's tone was dry.

Who was he that so many people had this reaction to him? I had yet to find fault with him, so perhaps he was traveling in the wrong circles.

A man joined Kirby. He was taller, closer to my own two meters. From what I was starting to understand, the shimmer around him—that I was starting to assume not everyone saw—meant he was a god. One without much power, similar to Bragi.

Magnus turned to me. "Nico, this is Kirby and Gwydion."

"Afternoon." I gave them both a smile and a nod. "I don't know if we've met before, but it's a pleasure to do so."

"You're the man with no memories?" Gwydion asked.

"Aye."

Kirby gave me a look that was half-smile, half-grimace, and all sympathy. "I'm sorry you're burdened with that."

"Come in." Gwydion opened the door wider.

Magnus entered first, and there was a staring match with Bragi and Gwydion that seemed to last an eternity, but was probably barely more than a second, before Bragi stepped inside as well. I followed them all into a living room with hardwood floors, and beautiful wooden furniture. Modern amenities were dotted through it, though. Television, speakers, and modern windows were placed to look like they were part of the classic decor, rather than a contradiction.

"You know what? No. I can't— Why is he here?" Kirby glared at Bragi.

Magnus twisted her mouth. "He has more information about Nico's past than anyone I know."

"Do you want me to go back and do things differently? I don't have that power, do you? Do you believe your life would've turned out better if I hadn't been involved? Just me?" Bragi said.

Kirby gritted her teeth and gave a half shake of head. "Fuck you, you manipulative, vile... *ugh*."

"Would you rather we leave?" I asked. This conversation wouldn't be productive if no one was interested in participating.

"No." Gwydion gestured to the seats in the room. "Sometimes we have to keep questionable company, and this is about you, Nico."

Magnus coughed, as if clearing her throat, and Kirby shot her a raised-eyebrow look.

It was fascinating to me how these women communicated with no words by default. I'd have to ask Magnus about it.

I sat on one of the sofas, and Magnus took the spot next to me, while everyone else settled as well.

"I've never met a phoenix before." Kirby's demeanor shifted toward fascination as she studied me.

I gave her a dry smile. "Neither have I. Not as far as I know."

She let out a short laugh. "Reincarnation humor. My favorite."

"Magnus tells me you've been through it—the reincarnation—several times," I said. "That you lost your memories each time?"

"I think of it more as taking a few decades to find them, but otherwise yes."

It was both comforting and frustrating to know I wasn't alone in this. Why did the universe offer a path like this? Though, every gift came with a price. "How? Or maybe where do you find them?"

Kirby glanced over her shoulder at Gwydion. "Usually with him."

That was hopeful.

"Do you hold onto them?" I gave my attention to Gwydion. "Is there a magical sort of box? Do you think I did something like that? Who would I ask? Where would I look?" The thread of excitement growing inside me at this news was unexpected, but I appreciated the glow. A tiny ember of hope in my chest.

"No." Kirby's answer didn't match my question the way I hoped. "I can't tell you exactly how it works, but I think the memories are always a part of me. The way I'm connected to Gwydion... There's something about the threads that bind us that means when I meet him, my memories are drawn to the surface."

Oh. "How would I discover if I had a bond like that with someone?"

"I'm a tool of fate." A hint of bitterness seeped into Kirby's response. "That's why those ties are there. You'd probably need to be the same."

"Not that she wants to be. Not that any of us do," Magnus muttered.

Kirby shrugged. "Sometimes it's better to recognize it than to try to fight it or second-guess it. You'll drive yourself insane if you spend your life trying to defy an ethereal concept you know maybe one percent about. But several of my lives brought me back to him. To the others. Do you have anyone like that—" Another choked laugh and shake of her head. "Sorry. You wouldn't remember."

"If there's anyone besides me, Nico never told me," Bragi said.

So maybe Bragi did have my missing memories. Or at least, the key to them. "Do you think that would work for me?" I wasn't letting go of this spark. "There are things about him, about Magnus, that are familiar. Could I be getting my memories back already?"

"Maybe? Reincarnation isn't as rare as we think, and I know of at least one other who had a similar experience, but recovering what's lost can't be forced. It happens when the universe wants it to happen." With Kirby's response, Gwydion got up and left the room.

Did we upset him?

Magnus let out a growl of frustration. "There's no way I'm taking *sit back and see what happens* as an answer."

"None of us can just sit and wait," Kirby agreed. "All I can do is tell you my experience and help you make some educated guesses."

"What's it like, having all those memories return at once?" I meant to save that question, but it slipped out.

The pain that crossed Kirby's face shouted with eons of agony, and then her sympathetic almost-smile was back. "It's hard to describe. I suppose it's like being surrounded by hundreds of TV's, playing every second of every TV show and movie ever, simultaneously. You can't process it all at once, but your brain grasps it. It's confusing. None of it is associated with anything else at first. It takes time to figure out which images and sounds and feelings go with which."

Her nostrils flared and she dragged in a deep breath. "Except the death. I know instantly, I remember every single time I died, and the pain that came with it. But that's part of my curse, so I don't think you'll have to deal with the same."

"I'm sorry." I didn't know what else to say to that.

"You experience that to a point, Nico," Bragi said. "I doubt it's as vivid as Kirby's, but you've told me when you come back to life, your previous deaths are like any other traumatic memory."

That sounded horrific.

I still wanted it, though. A week ago, I was a little frustrated to have no past, and couldn't accept that I may never. Then Magnus and Bragi showed up, and told me there was more to me than thirty or so years of missing experiences.

Sitting here, in this simple setting, surrounded by these implausible people, the impulse gripped me stronger than it had since I woke up with no memories—I desperately wanted to know what kind of lives I'd lived. That past was mine and I wanted it back.

"I wish I could help you more. You seem like a good guy." Kirby leaned back in her seat.

She must've known before we arrived that she didn't have answers. Why were we here? The abrupt revelation of wanting solutions came with a frustration that I was surrounded by stone walls keeping me away from them.

Inspiration struck. Now that I had a little more information, I was going to cram pieces together until they gave me a direction. Like Magnus said, I couldn't just sit back and do nothing.

"Do you know anything about recovering lost power?" If this process required someone who connected me to my past, and that person *was* Bragi, perhaps him becoming who he used to be would help me do the same. "Any of you? Not just Kirby."

"Mine comes back with my memories," Kirby said.

Magnus let out a long sigh. "Kirby gave me mine."

"I can really only do that with Valkyries, and it has yet to work on other magical creatures." Kirby pushed from her chair, and approached me. "I can heal, though. Would you like me to try?"

Magnus huffed, and turned on the couch to face me. "I should've tried that first. Eliminated all the options."

"Not me." Wait, what was I turning down? I didn't have nearly enough knowledge to rule out any option. "Rather, please, yes. Try healing me, unless it's going to kill me." I laughed, and was met with glares. Tough room. "But I meant for Bragi."

He grunted and pinched the bridge of his nose.

"I think he wants to keep that a secret." Magnus looked amused.

Right. No man wanted to admit he was impotent. "Apologies, but we're here for answers."

"I don't have any for him." Kirby reached toward me. "Your hand."

"I may have something." Gwydion was back, strolling through the room with a book in hand. "Finish what you're doing."

I placed my palm against Kirby's. The tingle was light at first, like a foot falling asleep, or when it was too hot under the covers. The odd sensation became unpleasant, then hot. Scalding.

Flame erupted around Kirby's and my hands where they met, and she jerked away with a sharp yelp.

The flame vanished the instant we broke contact. I wasn't damaged in any way, but she had fared worse.

Gwydion dropped the book and sprinted across the room. "Are you all right? What happened? Let me see." His soft demeanor was gone, banished behind a wall of surging and flickering power.

Kirby held up a scorched hand, similar to what Bragi's had looked like last night after touching Dahlia. As with him, Kirby's injuries faded in a blink. "I'm fine. But no, my magic isn't compatible with yours. I can't help beyond consultation, I'm sorry."

The glow of hope inside me flickered. It didn't die, but it was on shaky ground for something that had burned so intensely a short while ago.

CHAPTER 7

MAGNUS

When Kirby was trying to help Nico, the emotions that surged inside me were more potent and cloying than the air around a perfume counter in the mall. Hope. Trepidation.

When Nico and Kirby caught fire, the fear nearly choked me, as it mingled with disbelief. I was used to sifting through feelings and giving them names— it was part of how I survived and hid my feelings at TOM.

But these felt different. As if not all of it came from inside me. *Weird thought.* Where else would it come from? If these were my emotions just a couple of months into pregnancy, these muddled, uncontrolled *things*, I might want to put myself in isolation for the next seven or so months.

"Let me see." Gwydion was already at Kirby's

side, pulling her hand toward him. Examining her arm. Even if he weren't a doctor, I suspected he'd be doing this. I felt concern. Confusion. Protectiveness.

Of course I did, because this was an intense situation, and I didn't have any idea why things were unfolding this way.

"I'm fine," Kirby gave Gwydion a reassuring smile. "Magical Valkyrie healing powers, remember?"

"What about you?" I asked Nico.

He wore a deep frown. "I wasn't hurt. I'm glad your friend is all right. I didn't mean to injure anyone."

Guilt?

Did I feel that because I brought him here?

Yes, but mine tasted different.

"Well, that was fun." Kirby's voice was clear again. Matter-of-fact, with a large helping of let's-get-back-to-business. "You found something?" she said to Gwydion.

I didn't blame her for wanting to move on. There were no lasting injuries, and lingering in a crisis was dangerous.

Nico straightened in his seat. "I'm sorry. Is no one else concerned about the fact that I lit Kirby on fire?"

The sensation of confusion surged, but again, I didn't feel it myself.

This wasn't normal, was it? Anything we were

doing? It was in our world, but I could see how to Nico, to someone who hadn't been part of our lives, it seemed strange. "Like Kirby said, her magic doesn't always work with other magics. She can't heal Dahlia, either."

"Does Dahlia ignite when Kirby tries?" Nico looked at me in disbelief.

"No." Kirby lingered on the word. "But it's not pretty. It's more electric than helfire."

Nico let out a cough. "*Helfire*. Not sure how I feel about that."

"You dropped this." Bragi picked up the book from where it had fallen, and handed it to Gwydion.

Bragi must be so proud of us right now. Pretending every traumatic moment was as normal and expected as ordering a cup of coffee.

Gwydion took the book from Bragi, and looked at Nico. "I'd say you get used to it, but you really don't. They talk about it when they're ready."

Kirby smacked his arm playfully. "Hey now. No fair telling all our secrets." Her voice was light but strained.

Nico was right—we were fucked up.

Gwydion sat in an overstuffed chair, and opened the book. Kirby perched on the arm next to him.

I was always fascinated by and a little jealous of the dynamic between Kirby and the people she loved. She was in charge. Queen mother-fucking-Valkyrie. She'd been team leader in school. In an operation, she commanded with an efficiency and grace that was unmatched.

And behind closed doors, she wasn't interested. She let her loves take control the rest of the time.

What would it be like to trust a lover that much, let alone more than one of them?

And what would it be like if I could climb out of my own fucking head and pay attention to this conversation?

Gwydion was careful with the book as the heavy leather binding creaked open. He turned one thick page after another. "There's an old fairy tale—literally part of fae lore—and it's been centuries since I heard it. There's a version in here though. About an old spring that runs through their realm and can restore lost things."

"*Lost things* is vague," I said.

He nodded. "If it's vague in one of their stories, it's on purpose. It's meant to cover a lot of territory."

"I know this one." The way Bragi lingered at the edge of the throw rug made it clear he wasn't a part of the group. He looked like an outsider wanting to step in. Wanting to join but knowing he wasn't welcome.

Okay—where the fuck did those thoughts come from, and why did I feel the longing in them?

"Different retellings reference different missing items," Bragi said. "Power. Memories. Appendages."

That sounded like a neat trick. "So it can grow back a missing arm?"

"If you use it correctly." Gwydion flipped a third of the way through the book, and hovered his fingers above the pages with reverence.

"Then it's not just a matter of jumping in the water and making a wish?" Kirby asked.

Bragi leveled his gaze at her. "Is it ever?"

He had a good point, and it pained me to admit that. "I don't suppose that book has the steps."

"Yes... and no." Gwydion glanced at the pages.

Frustration surged inside, more potent than I was used to, and I lived through a lot of the stuff. Something lay underneath, as well. Disbelief? More than simple doubt, like the knowledge that this wouldn't work.

Was I so jaded I'd already written the thing off? I knew as well as any of these people that ancient texts may be deceptive and open to interpretation, but there was frequently a truth buried inside.

"It doesn't work." Bragi's words wove with the emotions I struggled with.

I glared at him. "How would you know?"

"Because there's a fucking prophecy that says I'll lose my power, and I researched everything I could find before it happened, to make sure I had a backup plan."

"So you actually used the spring." Disbelief bled from Kirby's statement.

Bragi gave a terse nod. "Yes."

Oh. Well, fuck.

"I also looked into transfers of power, both similar to what Kirby does and what Gwydion and Starkad did. I don't suppose either of those would work for memories, and if it did, my recollection of Nico telling me about his past isn't the same as him living it. I also looked into…" Bragi trailed off. "A lot of things."

Like the technique he used to restore my power after one of my last fights with Vidar. I understood why he wasn't talking about it—the last thing he needed to tell the people in this room was that he'd tortured me.

But this wasn't about Bragi, and Nico deserved to know what was involved, and allowed to decide for himself if he wanted to go through it.

"What about what you did for me?" I asked.

Disbelief and self-loathing surged inside, rising in my throat with bile.

That *definitely* wasn't coming from me. What the fuck?

"That's not for memories either," Bragi said. "You still had the power, and I could see the threads. I wouldn't have been able to access it otherwise."

"Do we know that Nico doesn't have the memories? You have to give him that choice." I didn't want Nico to suffer, but I needed him to get better. I needed—

"If I can't see them, I don't know if they're there. Can you see them?" Bragi countered.

Nico raised his hand with a single finger extended. "Excuse me. I'd like details."

Was that curiosity? I shouldn't feel that because I knew the answer. The apprehension was mine.

"I'd like to know too," Kirby said.

Gwydion closed the book. "Another vote makes it three."

Bragi sank into the nearest chair, leaving him at a distance from us. "It's not a fucking democracy. This entire conversation is ludicrous. No."

"Tell him for me?" I hated myself for the blatant and weak attempt at manipulation. Was it because I didn't put any effort into it, or because I didn't need to with Bragi, to get my way?

He gave me a blank look, but I swore I felt the conflict spilling from him.

I really needed to knock off this *feeling other's feelings* thing.

Bragi sat straighter and drew in a deep breath. "The concept is similar to what a guitar player does with callouses or a bodybuilder with muscle mass."

"Fuck me." As Gwydion spoke, disgust spilled through the room.

Not mine. I knew where this was going already. Apparently he did too, but I had time and personal experience, and he was just figuring out what Bragi meant.

"What?" Kirby asked.

Gwydion gripped the book, and his knuckles went pale. "He fractured her magical pathways again and again, and made them heal. How many times?" He directed a pointed gaze at Bragi. "How many microfractures?"

"Thousands," Bragi said.

They couldn't get mad at him for this. For a slew of other things, yes, but I owned this decision. "I gave him permission. He was up front about the process and consequences, and I agreed."

"But you weren't his first," Gwydion said. "Did the others agree?"

Bragi didn't flinch away from the accusing glare. "It's a magical procedure, and as I already said, it doesn't matter in this case because I don't know if Nico has the memories, and if he does, I can't see what's holding them back. I could see with Magnus."

His tone and posture were unapologetic. Disgust rolled around me, plus anger and fading hope. No one missed that Bragi didn't answer Gwydion's question. How was I feeling emotions from the others?

I couldn't be. That wasn't something I'd ever done before. Not beyond reading body language.

"I'd like to hear more about this magical spring—"

"Stream." Gwydion corrected Nico.

"Does it matter what I call it?" Nico asked.

Gwydion nodded. "Details always matter when it comes to the fae. Except when they don't."

That cleared everything right up. Though, it was my understanding that once upon a time Gwydion had dated fae royalty, so he probably knew better than most what to expect.

"It won't work." Bragi was all about shooting the ideas down today.

I was sick of it. "Why are you so determined to not help Nico?"

"I wouldn't be here if I didn't want to help." Bragi's voice turned hard. "That's why I want us to take the appropriate next steps." He was telling the truth.

But we had to do something. "We don't have any other direction right now."

"Magnus is right," Nico said. "What's involved with this magical stream? Would it really hurt to try?"

"It literally could, yes." Bragi leaned in and rested his arms on his knees. "There's a quest involved, and quests are rarely easy things. They're meant to filter out the chaff."

After everything we'd been through up to this point? Another quest should be easy. "We're hardly inexperienced novices. With most things."

Kirby hopped to her feet. "Magnus, can I talk to you in the other room?"

"Sure." I was curious about her less than subtle approach, but wouldn't refuse her. I followed her through a doorway opposite the entrance, and into a short hall that ended at a kitchen.

She paused between the two rooms and faced me. "You can't do this. You can't go with them."

"Like fuck I can't." I kept my voice low, to match hers.

Kirby looked at my stomach.

Right. I was living for three. I was also a warrior, both human and magical. "Tell me what I need to know about being a Valkyrie and being pregnant, and I'll be smart about this." I'd asked her this before and she'd put me off. I was tired of waiting.

"Valkyrie's don't get pregnant."

Obviously we did. "Never?" I let the disbelief spill into the single, flat word.

Kirby shook her head. "Odin made all of his Valkyries infertile, so before now... You're the first."

"I can't just sit back on my ass and wait for—" Hatred slammed into me. Definitely not mine.

From the next room, I heard the soft but distinct click of a hammer being cocked on a gun.

"This is a seventeen round mag. If I empty into the back of your head, do you die, or are you just inconvenienced for a while?" That was Brit, Kirby's girlfriend. Another woman we'd grown up with.

And I felt every bit of loathing and hatred she had for Bragi.

The emotions spilling through me were those of everyone around me. Somehow, though Bragi had lost his empathy, I had gained that same gift.

Curse?

But how? Why?

It didn't matter, because Brit would probably shoot him if we didn't get in there. Kirby and I were already sprinting back to the living room.

CHAPTER 8

BRAGI

I understood the animosity toward me, from any person I'd trained when they were students and I was the instructor, ten years ago. I wasn't surprised Brit's was more intense. At TOM, once it was determined which students were soldiers and which were the more elite Nobles, it was my job to teach them the finer points of *controlling* their feelings.

I wasn't always kind about it.

I also helped teach them the finer points of seduction. It was all at a point where I had lost myself in my empathy. It hurt too much to care, after centuries of drowning in the feelings of the people around me, I'd decided it was easier to revel in the pain, than suffer along with them.

Magnus broke my broken.

Most of those details didn't matter with the gun

Brit had pressed to the base of my skull. "I'd rather not see what I look like with my brains on the outside," I replied to her greeting.

"I said he could be here." Kirby walked into the room with Magnus next to her.

The barrel pressed harder into my skull.

"Agree to disagree," Brit said.

Magnus twisted her mouth and furrowed her brow. "Please?"

I'd do almost anything if she gave me that simple a plea, but that was me.

The weight vanished from the back of my head, and with a huff, Brit walked through the room, out the same door Kirby and Magnus had just returned through.

Silence blanketed the room.

I wouldn't sit here in awkwardness and wait for the others to shrug it off. I wasn't welcome here, and that didn't do Nico any favors in the gathering information department, so it was time to learn what we needed to and go.

If the next step in that was telling them the fairytale so we could move on to a real solution, so be it. "The story of the grieving seamstress." I spoke in a clear, loud voice, for dramatic emphasis. It had been too long since I got to share a sweeping tale with a group, and while this one wasn't mine, I was going to enjoy being the show. "Like most good stories, this one is about love."

"Star Wars isn't about love," Magnus muttered as she sank into her spot next to Nico again.

Did she really just compare ancient, refined literature to… I swallowed a sigh. "Star Wars is a love story to the Hero's Journey and merchandising rights."

One corner of Gwydion's mouth tugged up, and Magnus scowled.

I shrugged. "Different stories are about different loves. Sometimes the characters insist their tale be the focus, and other times the creator is the true subject. Do you want to hear this or not?"

"Yes." She rolled her eyes and made a show of clamping her jaw shut.

If I had my magic, I could weave a light illusion around the story. Make it come to life in a way that would draw the listeners in and wrap them up in the tale.

I'd have to settle for using words alone. "The heroine in our tale is a mother, a weaver, and formerly a wife. She adores her boys. When her husband leaves her, she doesn't have the heart to tell them that he abandoned his family. That he walked away from them and the life they'd all built together.

"Instead, she let them believe he'd lost his life to bandits, while traveling to another kingdom.

"Her sons were compassionate, and hated to see their mother in mourning. Grandmother used to whisper tales of ancient magic, and one of those stories told of a stream that could restore lost things. Since it was their father who was lost, they reasoned this could bring him back. It was actually their mother's heart that was lost, but we'll get back to that later." I winked at my captive audience.

Kirby didn't look impressed, but Nico watched me intently, not moving beyond a slow, even breathing.

"According to their grandmother, the items the boys would need were simple. A healing, cleansing salve, to purify the soul. To free it of cracks that would keep it from receiving what it needed. The next item was the finest drink, to soothe the heart. To calm it, so it could clearly state what it was missing. And a garment tied to wrap oneself in, after the bathing. To tie them to what's to come."

"That all sounds rather vague," Magnus said. "Who's to say I can't just head down to the giant store on the corner and buy some bodywash, some iced tea, and a new sweatshirt."

As far as I was concerned, that would be just as effective in this case. "I'm sorry, have you ever read a fairytale that turned out to be real?" I knew the answer was *yes. Of course.*

Magnus wrinkled her nose in response. "Fair enough. We'll do it the story's way. What happened after they gathered the items?"

I gave her a sweet smile, and continued. "They gift the items to their mother, and tell her *this will bring back Dad.* She's warmed by the gesture, but is forced to tell them, *your father didn't die. He left us for another woman. I don't want to bring him back.*

"Still, her sons have gone to all this trouble, and it's clear Mom needs something. Her oldest tells her *your heart is broken. Please, let this help.* She can't tell her sons *no.* She loves them and the gesture too much. So she follows the remainder of the ritual.

"While she's bathing in the stream, the grief and heartache sink in. In the solitude, she's free to think of how much it hurt to be betrayed, and she sobs until she can't sob anymore. She feels both drained and cleansed, and she finishes bathing. When she climbs from the stream, she's horrified to discover that someone—something—has run off with her clothes and the new robe. She doesn't know what to do.

"She's pondering covering herself with leaves, or shouting for help, and considering all the alternatives, when a woman approaches. *Is this yours?* The new arrival has the robe. *My pet fox brought it to me.* The new woman studies her, and asks if she's all right. With her pain so close to the surface, Mom breaks again. Spills out her heart. Empties her entire story into the forest, with only the trees, the stream, and the new woman to hear.

"The other woman is sympathetic. Takes her home. Makes her a real meal. The women fall in love.

Mom has her heart back, and the boys love the new woman. They all live happily ever after."

"Don't fairytales usually end with a cautionary message?" Kirby asked.

Not really. It was fun to see how people twisted them so, though.

"Is this one's message that if a man wrongs you, you'll turn gay for a nice woman?" Magnus looked like she was considering the implications.

"Sounds like my kind of story." Brit's voice carried from the next room.

Sometimes a tale was just a tale. "The point of this one, if you need a point, is that the real solution isn't always the one we want. In this specific case, if the stream were real, fate would interpret how it delivered its resolution."

"*I'd like my heart back* is far more open to interpretation than *I'd like the memories back that I had last time I died*," Nico said.

Everyone thought their request was straightforward until fate twisted their words. "I understand you don't remember, but everyone else in this room knows that words can be interpreted many ways."

"Can we fill out a contract first?" Magnus asked. "Make sure we cover the important loopholes?"

"It's not a djinn, it's a magic stream," Gwydion said.

The creator in me appreciated the idea of negotiating a desired outcome with a body of water. For all

I knew, the fae could make that possible. "There's nothing to contract, because this one isn't real."

"How long ago did you do it?" Nico's question tugged on my own memories. When we were together, he didn't give up. He clung to an idea, and he pursued it, always needing to know for himself how the tale ended.

Until he gave up on me.

Seeing that drive return in him, even in this subtle way, sparked something inside me. "Thirty years," I said. "I did this thirty years ago, but I had my power at the time. I don't know if we can reach the places we need to without it."

"We're resourceful." Magnus always had been.

Like Nico, her drive was one of the things that drew me to her. The other Nobles had it too. There was no way to excel in what they'd done without the push to be more. However, in each of them—Kirby, Brit, Dahlia, their peers—it manifested differently. In Magnus, there was a pureness to it. She didn't do it just for her, or the handful of people she'd picked to keep in her inner circle...

Magnus had always wanted to save everyone. Because they deserved it, and not because she wanted the glory.

That was what had drawn me to her, and also scared me for her.

"What were you asking the stream to recover for you?" Magnus asked.

I met her firm gaze. "My youthful optimism."

She snorted in disbelief and shook her head. "Fine, don't tell me."

But it was true, and I wouldn't argue it with her. I'd wanted to learn to love feeling again.

"I need to do this. I have to try," Nico said. "And if there's nothing else, this is where we start."

I'd offered my help, and given them my thoughts on their path. I wasn't going to walk away now. "I'll give you everything I learned during my process. May we borrow the book?" I asked Gwydion.

He held it out. "Is it fucked up that the one thing I trust you with is this?"

I gave him a humorless smile and took the tome.

We had exhausted our ideas for getting Nico's memory back, and the conversation died off quickly. The only exchange happening were the looks Kirby and Magnus kept giving each other, but without words, it was simply that language they spoke that I couldn't translate.

We thanked Kirby and Gwydion for their help, and Magnus shouted a *goodbye* to Brit, before we stepped outside. We strolled to the sidewalk and Magnus took my hand and Nico's, to take us back to her cabin.

I appeared in the new location, but Magnus and Nico were nowhere to be seen.

Concern bled in like a punctured artery.

Where the fuck did they go?

I didn't know where we were, but it wasn't Magnus's cabin. Once upon a time it was something. The stone wall with a doorway and no door, the vague impression of rooms behind it, were barely anything now.

Shock was painted on Magnus's face as she surveyed the area. "I didn't... How? Did he know?" Her questions were soft, as if she were talking to herself. "I must've been... Fuck."

"Are you all right?" I wanted to ask *what is this place*, but it was more important to make sure she was thinking straight first.

She shook her head roughly, and focused on me. "Yeah. I'm good. A little in shock. This is Bragi's house. Or it was."

"When. A hundred years ago?" Should I recognize it?

"Last month."

That couldn't be right. This place was ravaged by age. "Why are we here?"

"I don't know." Magnus's voice had gone soft again. "I was thinking about it, only a little. When Dahlia was having trouble controlling her powers she used to... I don't know." She wandered toward the entrance, and I followed.

It wasn't easy to see in the dark, with no moon, but there wasn't much to look at. What used to be the inside was a chaotic series of outlines, some square, others not, all fitting together like a puzzle.

How had this only been standing a month ago? There was no furniture or flooring. No shelves. No wall was higher than a few feet.

Magnus's steps were slow, as if she was reluctant to move one foot in front of the other. "This was the kitchen and dining room." She paused in the middle of one of the larger squares and pointed as she spoke. "Bedrooms. Study."

The last space she indicated had more of a silhouette than the other bits, and we started toward it. The corner we reached first had a different shape. A jacket? I picked it up, and Magnus let out a soft gasp.

How much of this should I recognize? Would I be sharing her reactions if any of it was familiar? I ached to know what that was like, despite the disbelief and grief splashed across her face.

"What is it?" Worn leather was soft against my palm as I handed the jacket to Magnus.

She held up her hands, palms out, and stepped back without taking it. "It's Bragi's."

That made sense, given where we were, but I had a feeling there was more to her reaction. I wanted to reach out and comfort her, but I didn't know for what.

Did it matter? She was distressed.

"Tell me," I prompted instead.

She reached for the leather, but didn't make contact. "I was struggling in training, and he loaned it to me. Told me some ridiculous story about how it was magic and would get me through anything. I knew it wasn't a magic coat, but I held onto it anyway. It meant more to me that he cared than the fucking thing having any sort of power. But I left it behind when I walked away from Vidar and TOM."

And now it was in the middle of this desiccated place, where no other things remained, aside from—

"Why are there stacks of paper in here?" Magnus moved into the room.

Those were the silhouettes we'd seen, and as we drew closer it became clear they were piles of pages torn from books. I grabbed several off the top of a nearby stack, and paged through heavy, aged parchment. "None of them are in order." One page ended and the next was picked up with a different tale and tone. There was so much *gone*. "Why?"

"Bragi has more enemies than friends, and his books are some of his most prized possessions." Magnus reached for another stack.

Heat and flame raced through my mind—not physical, but the impression of both. As her hand reached the pages, I saw a glow spread around the stack and several others. It was almost ethereal. Here, but not. In my head, but real.

"Stop." I grabbed her wrist, but I wasn't fast enough. She made contact.

Flame—real and hot without question—erupted around us.

"*Go,*" I shouted, as a fireball filled my vision. As with Kirby, the heat didn't cause me pain, but my heart slammed against my ribs as the barren landscape vanished, and we were in front of Magnus's cabin.

"What happened?" Bragi's barked question was a jarring backup to the chaos in my thoughts.

My gaze landed on Magnus again. Her clothing was scorched in several places, and deep, red welts on her skin were turning pink, then returning to her pale natural skin color.

"The jacket." She nodded at the clothing clasped tightly in my hand.

It was burned in several places as well.

"Where were you?" Bragi's tone was hard. "What happened?" He looked between us. "Are you all right?" Concern bled into his demanding question.

"We're fine. Nico warned me..." Magnus looked at me. "You knew something was going to happen."

"I sensed it. Saw, I guess, auras around the pages." I didn't have better words for the experience.

Magnus furrowed her brow. "Have you always been able to do that?"

I assumed she meant that I could remember. Had I? "I suppose? The world looked like it always does, with each object cast in its own glow, but there, I knew that it meant something."

"*What happened?*" Bragi's shout shook the air.

"We landed at your house." There was a hesitation in Magnus's tone with each response that made it sound like she wasn't certain of her words. "But it wasn't."

I struggled to believe that spot had been a home at any point recently. "Wherever we were, it was as if the place had been abandoned for centuries. Most of it wasn't standing anymore."

Magnus gave Bragi a look of sympathy, possibly even pity, that was a sharp contrast to the disdain she'd worn around him since I met them. "Did you know?"

"That my house was destroyed?" Bragi scoffed. "I was just in it a few days ago. It was fine. Fuck." He scrubbed his face. "And you both... There was fire? You're all right though. We need to go inside."

As we walked, I handed him the coat. "This is all that was left. I'm sorry."

He snatched it from my hands and looked at Magnus. "I thought you had this last."

"I left it behind when I walked away from TOM. Wait." She paused in her walking, and bent to pick up a scrap of paper that had just fluttered to the ground, from the coat. "What...?" She unfolded it, and paled.

"What is it?" After the strangeness we'd experienced, I had a hard time believing a brief note deserved any sort of reaction.

Bragi took it from her, and read. "*I know.*"

That was what it said? Or was he agreeing?

"Know what?" Magnus asked. "We assume that's from Vidar, right?"

"Not a clue to the first question, and yes to the second." Bragi jerked his head toward the house.

The instant we were inside, the door closed behind us, I let out my next question. "Can this Vidar do things like what we just saw? That place looked like ancient ruins."

Bragi sighed, hung the now-tattered jacket on a nearby hook, and looked at the note that had fallen from the pocket. "The elements weather things. You hit a new thing with the right elements hard enough, it will become an old thing."

That made a disturbing amount of sense, but, "Why would he do that?"

"The reason Vidar's path and mine have intersected so often is power," Bragi said. "My interest was in recovering what was lost, when I reached the point I'm at now—powerless. He was concerned with getting more. I can't say for certain, but I assume the note means he's aware I've lost mine, and reminding me he's stronger than ever."

"Not a lot of subtlety or metaphor there," I said.

Magnus wrinkled her nose. "Neither of those describes Vidar." She wandered to the futon and dropped onto the cushion with a heavy sigh. "Which is why I don't understand his approach here. He's spent all this time magical cyborging himself—"

"I'm sorry, what?" I hated to cut her off, but I needed more context. I took a seat next to her.

Bragi stood, but he reached for Magnus's hand. her entire body went rigid when he touched her, but she didn't pull away. "This." He singled out her middle finger.

I'd noticed the full-finger claw ring—the beautiful, ornate jewelry was impossible to miss—but I assumed it was a fashion choice. "What about it?"

"It's imbued with Dahlia's magic, and lets me do some of the things she can do as a dragon." Magnus took her hand back and nestled it in her lap. "And it's based on one Vidar enchanted for me. He's enchanted similar objects to a lot of his loyal followers, and he's done the same to himself, but on a massive scale. He's used various techniques to bind other magics to himself, but his aren't trinkets. He's made his enhancements a part of him."

He sounded dangerous. Not that I didn't think that before, but this... "Why is he so determined to kill you?"

"He's not." Magnus shrugged. "I'm not important—I'm no one. I don't have the power to stop him. I'm just an obstacle to him getting to Dahlia."

That sounded like she was the opposite of what she'd said. "If you're the only person standing in the way of someone else dying, that makes you the most important person there is."

"Arguable." Magnus didn't look convinced.

"And now you know which side I'm arguing."

"But Magnus's other point remains." Bragi must've heard something I missed. "Vidar's actions don't make sense. None of them."

Magnus held her hand in front of her, wiggling her fingers and causing the light to dance off the claw. "He knows where I am. He finds me every time I'm in the open. He knew..." She clenched her jaw.

"He knew she was with us, when she thought Dahlia was dead," Bragi said softly.

She glared at him with a venom that might poison the air if she held the look. "Because you lied to me."

Bragi raised his brows. "But Vidar lets you live."

"Kind of makes you wonder how much more powerful you are than he's let on." I couldn't be the only one who had figured that out.

Magnus shook her head. "I'm not, though. It's a

great thought, but if I am, I can't use it. I've been in fights for my life with him. Fights for her life and yours. *If* I had more, and I couldn't touch it in those moments, then it's useless."

"To you." I hated how callous that sounded. "I'm not being cruel, but see this from his perspective. If you can't use it, but he can…"

"Then he would've taken her," Bragi said.

Magnus pushed to her feet as if her body weight had doubled. "Vidar's not subtle, he's convoluted. And he's a fucking sadist. For all we know, he just likes watching me suffer, and curse his name in the process. Can we eat? I want lunch."

I didn't blame her for not wanting to dwell on the subject. There was more talking to do, though. Inspiration struck. "I'll make Alfredo, Bragi can make salad, and Magnus can help me dice and grate other ingredients?"

They agreed without tossing barbs at each other. It seemed lunch was the one thing Bragi and Magnus saw eye to eye on.

In the kitchen, the three of us moved around each other with little conversation. This was a small space, but there was a dance in the way Magnus gathered ingredients from the fridge, Bragi selected knives, and I prepped the cooking area.

The ballet of it all was stilted, as though neither of them wanted to be participating, but also smooth as though the dance came naturally.

"We've done this before," I said.

"We have." Bragi took the freshly washed tomatoes from Magnus.

She moved on to a bunch of parsley. "We played house for a while. But it was a lie." She cast a glare over her shoulder at Bragi.

"That part wasn't." He managed to sound both sad and abrupt at the same time, and never paused in dicing tomatoes.

So much for peace. I didn't want this conversation to degrade, but there were so many things we needed to discuss. So many answers we didn't have. Which topic was most likely to lead to solutions rather than Magnus and Bragi tossing accusations and glares back and forth?

"Will you tell us what happened when you used the magic spring?" I arranged pots and pans on the stovetop to begin cooking. "The one from the fairytale?"

Bragi set the tomatoes aside and moved on to carrots. "I already told you. Nothing."

"You're a storyteller." I heard it every time he let himself fall into a tale. When he wasn't intentionally holding back. "There's more to what you experienced than *nothing*."

"You don't want to hear this," Bragi said.

Magnus handed him the last of the vegetables. "We do." Her tone had gone from accusing to curious.

"Tell us what to expect. Wrap us in a stunning epic." I didn't have to be any sort of psychic or mind reader to guess that feeding his ego would help coax him. "If anyone can do it, it must be you. Unless there's a reason you don't want to share."

He shook his head and continued to slice. "I already agreed to help you. Why do you want to hear about the frustration, failure, and disappointment?"

I didn't have a reply. As much as I thought the details might help us, if that was truly the way he saw things, he'd be reluctant to give us much.

A lull in conversation settled over us as we worked, and the sound of utensils against cutting boards and pans occupied the space that talking should have.

"The entire experience was rather mild. As far as quests go, anyway." Bragi broke the silence.

I hid my smile at what sounded to me like the start of a story. This all felt familiar, like whispers of a dream that had flitted away upon waking. The making food, and the way Bragi began his tale. There was a hesitation in his voice, but it was reluctant. As if he didn't want to be reserved, but knew he should.

Or I was so desperate for some of this to hold a deeper meaning, that I was projecting my hope on the situation.

There was no harm in trusting my gut, though. I was going to push forward until I saw a reason to do otherwise. "No seduction or monsters?" I asked.

Bragi shook his head. "Not in the way you'd think."

"So we're not talking about raging psycho dream gods or sirens or anything?" Magnus's examples felt intentionally specific.

"Not a single one," Bragi said.

Magnus sliced a hunk of cheese from a larger block, for the grater. "If you don't want to talk about it, you shouldn't force yourself." Was that teasing in her voice? Playfulness?

Bragi let out an exaggerated sigh. "Neither of you will be happy until I tell you, so you might as well pay attention." He diced with a practiced hand. "To gather the cleansing salve, I journeyed to a far away land, to speak with an ancient, wise being."

"Ooh. Narnia?" Magnus looked at me. "He used to have a doorway to Narnia in his house."

I felt like that should mean anything to me. "I don't know what that is."

Bragi chuckled and set the remainder of his prepped food next to me, then turned to clean up his space. "It wasn't Narnia. The door went to a portion of the fae realm."

"Narnia was in a series of books. Bragi wrote them. I'll put them on my tablet, and you can read them, Nico."

There was an intimacy in the idea of sharing her favorite stories. "I'd like that."

"Ah, the dream of bookworms the world across.

Being able to re-read books as if it were for the first time." Bragi spoke with longing.

It was probably a delightful thing, but I wouldn't surrender what I was missing, just for that. "Where was this distant land?"

"Montana," Bragi said with a smirk.

Magnus tossed a dish rag at him. "I bet it wasn't even a fae who helped you. Fucking Montana?"

"She's an elf. She likes the wide open spaces, and the fact that she can get a great hamburger there."

"Elves and fae are the same thing, are they not?" Should I know that? "How do I know that?"

"Elves are the fae and their children who have been expelled from the kingdom," Bragi explained. "I assume you know it the same way you understand most basic things about the world. Whatever took your memories considered that to be core knowledge. Besides, Magnus, you have us hiding out in Wyoming, and you're turning your nose up at Montana?"

Something about his reaction to that one thing, amused me.

"I like wide open spaces and good hamburgers, with no people around." She stuck her tongue out. "Who the fuck is going to look for me here?"

Bragi gave a hard shake of his head. "That's disturbingly convenient, given this being can't be reached by magic. The area around her, for miles, isn't the kind of space you can blink in and out of.

You drive to a point, and make the rest of the journey on foot."

"Why do you have to drive there?" I didn't understand.

Bragi leaned against the counter. "Maeve doesn't like magic being cast near her borders, and that includes blinking in and out. It's a bad idea to piss off the powerful being you're asking for help."

"It's almost like it's fated that we do this." Magnus handed me a large bowl of grated cheese.

I mixed it into the cream sauce.

"You don't believe in fate," Bragi said.

She grabbed dishes and silverware from their respective spots and set the table. "I believe the universe works awfully hard to be a dick to us. It's settled. We'll go tomorrow and talk to this elf."

Bragi stepped in to help me mix the final ingredients. The way his shoulder pressed to mine was warm and familiar in this tight space.

Damn it, I wanted to know where each of these whispers of intimacy came from.

"I'll go tonight. Alone," Bragi said.

The plate Magnus was holding hit the table with a heavy *clang*, and she fixed him with a stare of disbelief.

Bragi sighed. "She's not going to see me if I bring anyone with me. If you want my help, you have to trust me."

Like that, the feeling in the air shifted, and

Magnus furrowed her brow. "That's the problem, isn't it? I don't. I can't trust you."

Bragi frowned. "I know." His nostrils flared. "I'm here of my own volition. Not for kicks, and also not because you forced me to stay. If I want to leave, I can leave. If I want to go hop a flight to New York, I don't need your permission. We're doing this—I'm doing this—to help, and bringing either or both of you with me, will jeopardize that."

He made a series of good points that were hard to counter.

Magnus worked her jaw, and sighed.

"I'm going to need a car," Bragi said.

He made reservations, and the three of us ate in an awkward silence punctuated by Magnus occasionally scowling at Bragi, and him pointedly looking way. He didn't eat much before he pushed back from the table, thanked me for the meal, and said he needed to go if he was going to reach his destination at a time when he could be seen.

Magnus didn't look happy about it, but she blinked him to the car rental place, and was back in an instant.

I wanted to distract her from her unpleasant mood, and more importantly, I wanted to see her smile. That impulse ran deep. I led her to the couch, and pulled her to sit next to me. "You're doing all of this for me, and I can't remember anything about you. Tell me about you," I prompted.

CHAPTER 10

MAGNUS

I didn't like this. Having no idea how to keep both Dahlia and my children safe. What Vidar did to Bragi's house. Me sitting on my ass in the middle of nowhere, with no idea how to act or where to turn next, and relying on a man I swore I'd never trust again, to get us to next steps.

I should be doing something. *Anything*.

Anything besides waiting, that is.

Settling in next to Nico was a nice distraction. It didn't clear away my anxiousness, but it did smooth the rougher edges. He wanted to know about me, and I wanted the same from him. Right now only one of us was capable of offering that information, and at least it meant I was taking action.

"What do you want to know?" I asked.

"Tell me the first thing that comes to mind."

In other words, sift through the chaos of

thoughts, and pluck one out that wasn't *why aren't I destroying Vidar at this very moment and restoring you to who you were.* "I love Star Wars."

Confusion spread across Nico's face. "Is that aliens fighting in space? Is it literal stars doing battle?"

"It's a series of movies." I couldn't help but smile at his ignorance, though it was one of the things frustrating me. Seeing the world through his eyes was a unique and fun experience.

"A series of movies about literal stars engaged in battles?"

I smiled. "I suppose technically there are aliens and spaceships. But it's about a normal boring orphan, living on a big ball of sand."

Nico glanced toward the windows. "Like here?"

"Not as many mountains or as much scrub brush in the movies. But then they find out—"

"They?"

"There are three trilogies and each one has a different sand orphan." Damn it. "I'm not doing the best job at explaining why I love them."

Nico faced me, placed a finger under my chin, and turned my head toward him. "You're perfect at explaining it. You have a little smile on your face that's stunning."

Heat flooded my cheeks. Sure, I'd learned all the lessons in attitude and flirting and molding myself to any situation, but this kind of genuine sincerity... I'd never been good at shrugging that off.

"What do the sand orphans do?" Nico asked. "Do *they* fight in the stars?"

"Technically, yes. But more specifically, they find out they have access to a power called The Force, which is kind of like magic, but they don't call it that, and they take on an evil emperor." I'd never described the movies that way before, and now that I was... Holy fuck, how did it sound so much like my own life?

As much as I loved the films, I hoped fate had written me a better script. I turned more of my body toward Nico, so my knee rested against his, and I could look him in the eye.

"They win, I assume. The sand orphans beat the evil emperor," Nico said.

"In the best movies, the good guys always win." Maybe that was why I liked those specific films so much. It was clear who was good and who was bad, and good triumphed. Kirby and Brit would tell me I was being naive, but I loved the idea. Mostly because in the real world...

I couldn't finish the thought, but it made me frown.

"What's wrong?" Nico searched my face.

"In the real world, sometimes the bad guys win, and that sucks."

He rested a hand at the back of my neck, and

pulled me closer as he leaned to press his forehead to mine. It was a simple touch, but it sent warmth and assurance flowing through me. "They won't win this time." He sounded so certain.

I didn't know how he could be. "I hope you're right."

"I know I'm right, because I've never met anyone as determined and driven as you."

His certainty combined with reality and my laugh tore out without permission. I straightened up, breaking the contact between us. It wasn't that what he said was funny, but my brain twisted it and found the humor in his words. "The only people you remember meeting, besides me and Bragi, live in a tiny village on a small island. Some of those people are pretty driven, and a lot of them worship the old gods, but even then, I don't think that's a big enough sample size to compare me to."

"It doesn't matter. I stand by my statement." Nico slipped his hand under mine, and lifted both, extending my middle finger and putting my claw ring on display. "Can anyone get a ring like that? That seems pretty handy. Are there magical gift shops where I can pick one up?"

Was this a better topic than evil ruling the world? I wasn't sure, but it seemed like it. "Magical beings are stingy when it comes to sharing their power. The jewelry has to be gifted out of selfless love, and there's a shortage of that in the world. " It was one of the tricks Vidar used with the trinkets he'd given us, when we were Nobles. He used tainted blood magic to imbue gifts we'd received from others. That was his loophole for the *gifted with love* requirement.

"You have one, though. That proves how special you are."

"I don't know why you're heaping on the praise." I both loved it, and was suspicious. Sincerity wafted from him like the scent of freshly baked cookies. Warm. Delicious. Attracted to me.

Okay, so that last one wasn't like the cookies. The entire blend was wonderful and strange. The fact that I felt him. It made the entire conversation more intimate, but knowing what was in his heart almost felt like cheating. Like I was breaking some sort of rule.

"I'm being honest," Nico said. "I get the impression you don't see a lot of that."

From Dahlia. From my friends, but, "No, it hasn't been the standard in my life. I don't think it is for most people."

"That's a shame. The world needs more honesty." He put my hand down, but didn't let go, tangling his fingers up with mine instead. "Tell me more about you. It's not my life, but it's fascinating."

How was I supposed to meet an expectation like that? "I'm a natural redhead. Carpet matches the drapes." I pushed out a laugh, to keep him from taking me seriously, and fumbled for a better answer.

When Nico reached up and separated a strand of my hair from the rest, my breath caught. He wrapped the hair around his finger, and his fingers brushed my scalp. All of those things I felt from him zinged through me like I'd chugged his emotion.

It should be too much, but it was one of the most erotic sensations I'd ever experienced. Like a full body rubdown in the blink of an eye, that left my nerves tingling and my skin wanting.

"May I kiss you?" Nico's soft question echoed loudly in my head.

Had I ever been asked that? I licked my lips. "Yes."

His kiss was gentle. The barely-there brush of his mouth over mine, with no demand in his touch.

What spilled from his heart was different. Potent. Conflicted. He wanted to push for more. Wanted me as badly as I did him. But his own lack of knowledge held him back.

The onslaught spilled through every place he touched me, filling my senses and thoughts, until the deluge of feelings was terrifying. Suffocating.

I broke away, struggling to keep my reaction from surfacing. "I..." I wouldn't say something as cliche as *I can't*, but there was no other way to explain it. Whatever it was that let me feel other people, it had better be temporary, or I wouldn't be able to fuck, or even kiss, ever again.

How did Bragi survive this for centuries? Why would he want it back?

"It's okay." Nico slid his hand to my cheek.

His conflict was back, clashing with mine. I wanted to break away, but I also wanted to feel those bits of him that were sincere. That kept me wrapped up in him.

He pressed his lips to my forehead so sweetly, I nearly choked on the sugar. This feeling could consume me in a heartbeat if I let it. His adoration would easily wrap me in a ball of flame, and I'd be my own phoenix.

I needed to step away from the edge of that hole. I tried to be subtle, gentle, about breaking the contact between us, but I still felt his twinge of hurt curiosity.

"We should watch Star Wars." I managed to keep my suggestion from sounding too bright and forced.

"All right." Now Nico was confused.

I didn't like these sensations at all. I should ask Bragi about it. Or see if Dahlia, Fen, or Frey could point me to a resource.

Going to Dahlia was dangerous, though. Not that I could avoid her forever, but after Vidar's threat... I hated the idea of avoiding her, and hated even more the idea of losing her.

Bragi really did make the most sense, with this

being about empathy as far as I could tell. But would I get a real answer out of him? Even being able to recognize if he was lying didn't mean I'd know what the truth was instead.

Fuck it, I'd do my own research. I knew where to look online, and how to tell the bullshit from the ancient tomes translated into a modern text. I was brilliant and uncovering information.

Tomorrow.

Tonight, even if I needed to make sure I was careful with Nico, I wanted to spend the evening cuddling with him and watching my favorite movies. Seeing him react to something new to him.

And wondering what was going on with my head. I wouldn't be able to avoid those thoughts, no matter how much I wanted to.

CHAPTER 11
BRAGI

I'd spent the last several weeks with only me and myself for company. After less than forty-eight hours with Magnus and Nico, I dreaded the notion of being alone with my thoughts again.

This was a waste of time. I hadn't told Magnus and Nico that because I was cruel, or to stop them. I wanted the two of them to succeed. Driving down this freeway in the dark, with no company other than the occasional pair of headlights from truckers I passed, I couldn't help but flash back to the last time I'd done this exact thing.

It wasn't as if bathing in the stream, or collecting the items before then, would hurt anyone. It would consume our time, and I suspected that was what Magnus needed more than anything. Regardless of what she believed, I would do anything for her or Nico.

And while we were using this to keep our hands busy, our minds could be working on the appropriate solution.

The emptiness outside matched the space in my head where emotional noise usually lived. It was disconcerting and wrong and I didn't like that it gave my thoughts room to expand, like bubbles growing unchecked. Fragile, easily obliterated, but so numerous many replaced one over and over.

I shook the thoughts away. According to my clock and trip mileage, I was maybe an hour out from the next leg of my journey. Only one more hour of telling myself not to think. Not to remember. Not to dwell or fall into some misplaced sense of guilt. I'd done what I needed to, back then. Every step of the way, I did what was required of me by me.

What else could I replace the meandering with, though? Thoughts of Vidar? Of my apparently obliterated home?

I assumed the note—*I know*—was a reference to my missing powers. Not a big surprise there, that he'd have figured it out. The only reason we were allies to begin with was to learn how to defeat our individual prophecies, so I knew his as well as he knew mine.

Another reason to visit Maeve was to ask about Vidar. She hadn't been willing to share that information in the past, but this was another opportunity to try. She'd consulted with both of us, about power and acquiring it and retaining it.

From the outside, it might seem as if her helping anyone who could pay was a form of evil. She wasn't. She didn't have the same investment in day to day humanity that mortals did, but even when she gave out information, she wasn't reckless about it. She didn't help with destruction or death or chaos.

She trusted the people she worked with to do the right thing with the knowledge she provided.

The time passed more quickly than I expected, before I was pulling over to the side of the road, and parking my rental car behind a rocky outcropping.

I shut off the engine and the headlights, and let darkness and silence wrap itself around me. This far out, in the middle of nowhere, the main light was from the stars and moon. But it was overcast tonight, and that left me swimming through the pitch black.

A shiver sped through me as I stepped into the open air. I wasn't safe out here until I crossed the invisible border into Maeve's. I'd be protected by her magic, by the shell that required anyone in her territory to play nice.

Until then...

If anyone was looking for me, Vidar for instance, I was a sitting duck.

My eyes adjusted to the blackness enough for me

to make out shapes, and I headed toward a patch of juniper bushes. The fact that the lush green plants grew in the middle of a dry, desolate desert, was a good indicator this was magically monitored land.

As I reached a hand into the shrubbery, needles pricked my skin and bark chewed at my flesh. I extended my fingers, searching for a different text. Feeling for—

There it was. I tightly grasped the worn wood handle, and tugged the tin lantern free.

The instant I touched it, a soft glow emitted from the object. Barely enough to make itself seen, but it would grow brighter as I worked my way toward Maeve's.

Something pierced my shoulder from behind, and pain tore through me. I dropped the lamp, and couldn't bite back my scream.

What the fuck?

Another spear drove through my thigh, this time I could see the ice glisten in the weak glow from the ground, before the weapon evaporated in wisps of cold.

A shadowy figure stepped in front of me. "You're a hard man to track down."

Probably because until I'd lost my power, I preferred to stay hidden in another realm, away from people and their feelings.

My wounds weren't healing—this was a magical attack.

Considering he'd pierced me with instantly evaporating ice, that was a *well duh* kind of moment.

"Did Vidar send you?" I needed something to say, and that flew to the tip of my tongue.

He spat on the ground. "As if I'd ever do anything for that vile— You don't know who I am."

"Should I?" One thing I *shouldn't* be was so flippant, however, I recognized most by their emotional signature and I couldn't feel that anymore. He attacked me without warning—why the fuck would I give him consideration?

His roar told me I'd given the wrong answer, and another attack pierced my side, knocking me back, and pinning me to the ground until the weapon vanished. Then another. And another. A rain of ice spears driving through me one after another until I was on one knee, gasping for air and struggling with consciousness.

"Hel used to do a trick like this. She'd be disappointed you're not better at it." I should be quiet now. However, if he didn't like Vidar or me, there was a good chance he was a student, and hated her too. Taunting him would either earn me another wave of pain, or piss him off to the point of distraction. I was willing to gamble.

"*Shut up.*" His roar shook the ground. "You're always talking. Taunting. Why the fuck can't you shut up?"

It was a curse sometimes, really. "You're obviously here to take out your frustration. If I stayed silent, would that help?"

His angry shout didn't tell me if that was the right answer or not. "Just tell me where Magnus is."

Maybe I should know this man. It wasn't easy to make out features through the darkness and pain, but I squinted and tried.

Nope. I was certain he hadn't been a Noble, but if he was familiar with me, he'd been in the running. If he was wielding this kind of power, that also meant Vidar had incorrectly read what kind of threat he'd be. There was a level of satisfaction in that knowledge.

I'd be smug when I wasn't being torn to shivering pieces. "Why would I know where Magnus is?"

"Because you never left her alone. Everyone saw it. You creepy, obsessive old fuck." Another wave of attacks, and I had to be full of holes at this point.

There really was a point where the pain became a big blur of numb. Would I survive something like this?

"You're a friend. I understand that. I could call Magnus. You could talk to her."

"None of your bullshit tricks and manipulations." He grabbed his head and shook it hard. "Stay out of my mind. *Stop*."

If something was in his head, it wasn't me, but I was a bit concerned about what *was* making him think I was poking around in his skull. "Where did the power come from? You're obviously strong. A warrior."

"I'm half Jotun. Which you know."

It was absolutely news to me. Now that I could see how unstable he was, my biggest hope was to hold out until Maeve got pissed off about the magic so close to her border, and showed up to expel him. I certainly wasn't bringing Magnus into a fight like this. "I didn't know. I swear it."

"*Stop lying.*" He summoned another wave of spears.

He must have a limit. I was certainly reaching mine, to the point where I didn't know if the blackness licking at the edges of my vision was unconsciousness or the night. The knee that was holding me up gave out, and I fell back, not catching myself on my hands before my head struck the ground.

"Johnny." That was Magnus's voice, and she didn't sound happy. "What do you want?"

I'd be amused that he'd done something more than I had, to piss her off, but I hurt too much.

"I've been worried about you," he said.

"I could've gone the rest of my life without seeing you, and it wouldn't be long enough," Magnus replied.

Johnny gave a short laugh. "Don't kid like that. A guy might take you seriously."

Another spear flew at me, and I flinched. It never connected. My consciousness slipped, and I would grasp it back, as Magnus and Johnny talked and argued.

I couldn't help her, and I hated that. I couldn't even stay awake.

"*How dare you fight at my borders?*" There was Maeve. She gasped. "It's you."

Which one of us?

I wanted to ask. I couldn't sp—

CHAPTER 12

MAGNUS

When I got Bragi's call, I had a feeling it was basically a butt-dial. He wasn't on the other end, and all I heard was scuffling.

Until he screamed.

I didn't want to feel the impact of that sound. I didn't want to care.

And fuck it, I did anyway.

I disconnected and looked up to find Nico watching me, concern splashed across his face. "What was that?" he asked.

"Bragi's in trouble."

"You should go. Unless it's Vidar. Then you can't go."

I didn't drop everything for that man. Bragi didn't deserve it. So why was I already forming a plan to prepare me for whatever I might be walking into? "I can't leave him. He's all but helpless right now, and he's there because I pushed for this."

It could be dangerous though. Nico was right. Was it Vidar?

There was a lot of weirdness about the call. The scuffling first. The scream. It could be a plan to bring me running. Was Vidar that much inside my head? He had to know there were a billion better ways to get me to come out than attacking Bragi.

Like picking on the night cashier at the convenience store down the street from NEON. She was always kind and chatty.

It didn't matter. Bragi was out there because of us. I'd go alone because apparently Vidar always knew where I was and could pick me off at any time anyway, and I'd hope it was someone else.

"I have to go after him," I said to Nico.

"I know. Do you want me to stay inside and not open the door for anyone but you?" His smile was tinged with concern.

I would've laughed if I didn't share his worry. "Something like that."

Nico loosely grasped my hand and kissed my fingertips. "Come back safely."

What a simple blessing, and one that warmed me to my core. I stepped from the cabin and sprinted beyond Dahlia's borders, before blinking to place Bragi had shown me he was going to cross a different magical border.

"Get up and fight back." The voice that greeted me when I arrived was enough to make my gut twist in on itself.

I felt like I'd been blindfolded, it was so dark here. A faint glow about ten meters away drew my attention, and by the time I registered it, I was already reacting. Flying toward the source, Valkyrie armor in place.

"Johnny," I barked his name as I reached them. I'd lost count of the number of times I'd told this fucker to leave me alone. This was the last thing I wanted to be dealing with right now, but at least I was pretty sure Vidar had nothing to do with him being here.

In the barely-here light, I couldn't see more than silhouettes, but that was enough to know that both figures looked in my direction when I touched down.

And one of those was crumpled on the ground, barely moving.

"Magnus." Johnny had the nerve to sound happy to see me. Though the glow, which appeared to be from a lamp on the ground, was a hazy yellow, his skin was so pale, it almost glowed white. "You *are* alive. Oh, my God. I've been so worried."

Uh-huh.

The feeling that radiated from him was anything but concern. Irritation was in there. Rage. A cloying desire for control.

On the other hand, what I felt from Bragi was fear. For me.

"I could've gone the rest of my life without seeing you, and it wouldn't be long enough," I said to Johnny.

He was one of Dahlia's and my best friends when we were teenagers. When he was kicked out of the Nobles program, he turned cruel. He would accuse me of fucking the instructors for my position, and reminded me over and over that I wasn't a good enough fighter to wear the title of *Noble*.

Johnny gave a short laugh. "Don't kid like that. A guy might take you seriously." He glanced over his shoulder at Bragi, and a spear formed in his hand. He fired it casually.

I tossed a magic shield up between Bragi and the spear, before it could connect with him. At the same time, I used a similar invisible wall to shove Johnny away from us. "I'd like if you took me seriously. That's the only thing I'd like you to do. Take me fucking seriously."

Back in the day, I'd been so hurt when he pushed me away. He was such a nice guy, I must've done something wrong.

I hated how badly Hel let us fuck with each other's heads.

Johnny had *forgiven* me, which at the time, I wanted. We were friends again, until I had a mission go bad. I needed someone to vent to, and

Dahlia was in the infirmary. I opened up to him, told him all how horrible it was, and he whipped out his dick and told me I'd feel better if I sucked him off.

He'd seemed genuinely astounded I was upset, and said, *I've been so nice to you. You owe me.*

"I've been worried sick about you," Johnny stepped toward me, and I used the Valkyrie magic shield to nudge him back. "I thought they hurt you or worse. But look at you. Are you a Valkyrie? Yet you still come at *his* call? What has he done to you?"

That was a fair question. Not coming from him, but it collided with demands I'd made of myself, for answers. I *did* run out here to save Bragi. Only hesitated for strategic reasons. What made him any different from Johnny?

Johnny was nice to me, thinking it meant I'd fuck him.

Bragi lied to me, thinking it meant I'd fuck him.

But the second one wasn't true. Bragi lied to me to keep me. Still disturbing, but he pushed me away so many times when I was with him. To the point where the frustration had devoured me.

"I don't owe you answers any more than I owe you anything else." I shoved Johnny back another step before he could get closer.

"Just tell me what you want." A cajoling, patronizing—he thought soothing—tone leaked into his voice. But under it all I felt frustration. Anger. A sharp slice of *make her pay.* "What do you need? Anything. I just want you to be happy."

Even if I couldn't feel the disgusting sludge of emotions oozing from him, I was no longer the lost, hurt little girl who needed that kind of attention. "What do I need to be happy? For you to go. The fuck. Away. How many times do I have to say it?"

"*How dare you fight at my borders?*" A voice rolled through the night, shaking the ground under my feet and vibrating enough to steal my breath and make my heart stall. A woman appeared between us, bathed in a pale, white glow.

In this light, it was clear the tint on Johnny's skin was bluish. Not that I cared why.

The new arrival was stunning. Delicate features. Angry, cold eyes that captivated.

And she was quiet. Her emotions. I couldn't feel them.

That was as lovely as she was.

She met my gaze and her eyes grew wide. "It's you."

Was that good or bad? I hated to confirm without knowing, but I was technically me. Should I say something? It may be safer to let her make assumptions and then go along with it.

This had to be the woman Bragi was looking for, which meant I needed to defer, to get what we were here to get. "I'm so sorry, great one." When in doubt, fall into worship mode. I should thank school for that lesson. I dropped to one knee. "This man attacked my friend, who was here alone to see you. I know how protective you are of your borders, and I apologize, but I can't leave a friend to suffer."

That was easier to say than I wanted—calling Bragi *friend*. Then again, I was a practiced liar.

"I see." Fury rolled from the woman in waves as she turned to Johnny. "You heard the Valkyrie." Her voice was both beauty and the promise of punishment. "Take her words to heart with everyone you meet. Leave her and never darken her doorstep again."

With that, Johnny was gone.

Holy shit. Just like that? "What did you do?"

The terrifying aura faded, and she turned to me with a playful smirk. "Exactly what I said. Small charm that forces him to accept your meaning. Basic stuff. My kind doesn't like liars, whether they're willing to admit to themselves or not that's what they are."

"Neat trick." I liked her. I should've asked Bragi to let me come in his place.

Fuck. *Bragi.* I pointed at his crumpled, unconscious form. "He was here to see you. I promise he was going to come alone. But there was a phone call, and a fight, and then that asshole you just sent away, and—" I had no idea how to convey everything in a short enough frame of time for it to make sense.

Dahlia would be able to do it.

The thought flitted through my mind on a distasteful blend of adoration and envy.

"I see." She didn't so much walk toward Bragi as float, though it didn't look like her feet left the ground. She knelt next to him and brushed a hand over his face. In the soft glow she cast, I saw blood streaked across his shoulders and neck. Soaking portions of his shirt.

Was I allowed to care? Was that fucked up that I didn't want him to be hurt on my behalf? Nico wouldn't want this either.

"I'm Maeve, by the way." She glanced back at me. "I don't know if he told you that. He's not supposed to. Grab his bag, will you, Magnus?"

She knew my name. Should she? Did he tell her or was it another elf trick?

All questions that could wait until Bragi was out of danger. I grabbed the backpack that lay a few meters from him.

Maeve picked up the lamp that was the source of the faint yellow glow, and it vanished. She reached her hand toward me, and I took it.

In a blink, we were inside. Bragi was in bed and Maeve and I stood next to him. The room was sparsely decorated, with a bed, dresser, and night-stand, and not much else. A patchwork quilt covered portions of the sleeping Bragi, but he had kicked off some of the covers.

In the normal light, indications of his wounds

were severe. His clothing had holes torn in several spots, all of them smeared with drying, pooling blood. It looked like Johnny had used him for sword practice. Or ice spear practice, based on the attack I witnessed.

I shouldn't be this worried about him, but sick concern boiled inside. "I can try to heal him." Valkyries could heal each other and mortals, but from what I'd seen with Kirby, it tended to be hit or miss when it came to using our magic on other immortals. "If it doesn't work, will you...? Can you? I'll pay. Trade. Whatever is needed."

And now I was bargaining on his behalf. He was here because of me. Because of Nico.

The glow vanished from around Maeve, and what I'd thought were flowing, sheer robes disappeared as well. The woman in front of me was still pretty, but instead of an otherworldly being, she was dressed in a lavender peasant blouse and a light-weight, wrap-around skirt.

She pulled up her sleeve, unstrapped a dagger from the holster wrapped around her forearm, and stepped toward Bragi.

"Whoa." I moved between them. "What the fuck?"

"His clothes need to come off, at least his shirt, to see what kind of treatment he needs."

Oh. Right. My head was all over, and half those places weren't smart ones. "How can I help?"

"Hold the fabric taut."

I did what she said, and she sliced away Bragi's shirt. I had no idea what I was looking at beyond *ouch*. And wishing I'd done some damage of my own to Johnny.

"He's already healing." Maeve wiped her blade on a clean bit of his clothing, and sheathed the weapon again. "He needs time, and then he can get cleaned up."

Okay. Good. In the meantime, "You recognize me."

That knowing smile of hers was back. She liked being the one with the information.

Noted.

"I knew your mothers, and you look just like Eira. I didn't think I'd ever seen you again."

Maeve's words knocked the air from me and blanked my thoughts. It took me a moment to recover. Someone knew where I'd come from. She was standing right in front of me.

This was a whole lot of wow to deal with at once.

"Let's go in the other room. Let our friend rest." Maeve pointed to the door. "I'll answer all your questions that I can."

"What will it cost me?"

She shook her head. "Not everything has a price."

Untrue in my experience, but I'd play things her way for now.

We walked through a living room that looked far more personal than what I assumed was the guest room. Small paintings and macramé adorned wooden walls, and a colorful rug covered most of the floor. A few large chairs sat in front of a current unlit fireplace.

The kitchen was small, barely more than an oven, fridge, and sink, and we sat at a table barely big enough for three chairs.

"I'm not used to your kind of visitor, so I'm afraid I'm not prepared. I can make you some tea. I think I have cookies or crackers, if you'd like." In this cozy setting, with the simple decor and the warmth that radiated through the cabin, Maeve was no longer a terrifying force. She reminded me more of a kind mentor.

Not that I had experience with such a thing, but I had a decent imagination. "I'm okay, thank you."

"All right." Maeve took a few steps toward the kitchen, then turned toward me again, and pulled out the chair across from me, to sit. "I didn't think you'd survived. I'm not sure where to start."

At the beginning. Tell me everything. Who I am. Where I came from. Why TOM wanted a nobody like me compared to basically guaranteed greats like Kirby and Dahlia. The only reason I had any power was because the two of them had gifted me, and even that wasn't consistent these days.

But this visit hadn't been planned on my behalf,

and as much as I wanted to know about me, if I had to pick, I would pick Nico's past. "Bragi came here to ask you for a salve. To help recover memory."

"For you?"

I shook my head. "For a mutual friend."

"Then when Bragi recovers, he can do what he came here to do. With him, it's business. You're the daughter of old friends, and that's different."

"Who am I?" I was being selfish, but she'd just given me permission, and I wanted so badly to know.

"Aiofe and Eira—your mothers—were witches. Mortal ones. I'd known Aiofe's family for generations."

Wait. "Known? Past tense?"

"She was the last of her line. Until you."

But I didn't know anything about them. I wanted to ask so many questions. Where was my family from? Who were my grandparents? Did they all practice magic? How did my mothers meet? How did they have a baby?

I didn't ignore the questions, but I would wait until Maeve was done with the basic story, to ask for more. "Was I theirs? As in, was there a sperm donor?"

"I never asked." Maeve shook her head. "That was between them. I was friendly with them, but not a friend. Rather, I was the midwife. When Eira was pregnant with you, we thought it would be twins, which were common in both families. I heard two heartbeats. Saw two auras." She looked me over.

She knew I was pregnant. I couldn't say how I was so certain, but she saw it.

"The second heartbeat vanished early on." Maeve continued the story. "Not as in the other twin died, but it was as if they were never there."

"Oh." I would've had another sister? A blood one? Would I have known her, given how I grew up? Was it better there was only me? I couldn't hold back all the questions anymore. "Why did they leave me?" I didn't mean to let so much angst slip into my question.

Maeve reached across the table to cover my hand. "It wasn't their choice. I promise they both wanted you. They both loved you even before you were born. But Aiofe was killed before that happened."

"How? Why?"

"I wish I had more details for you." Maeve sounded sincere. "But I suspect it was related to the fact that Hel's soldiers came for you right after you were born. Eira hid you both from everyone, including me. Until tonight, I never learned how successful she'd been."

"Not very. I don't remember my mother." A fact I'd gotten used to long ago, but now it ached.

She furrowed her brows. "I should've guessed. If

you know Bragi, I assume Hel found you at some point." Maeve furrowed her brows.

Falling into my childhood had always hurt, and mixing what I'd lived with this new information didn't make it better. This was so much to absorb. "I lived in the foster care system until TOM found me around my thirteenth birthday."

"I'm sorry." Maeve's frown deepened. "Eira hid from everyone. If I'd known... I'm sorry."

It was odd to have this stranger be more sympathetic about my past than most of the people I'd known in my life. Dahlia cared, of course. Nico might if he had any idea. Bragi did, and I hated being aware of that fact.

"It's okay, and it's not your fault," I said. "I want to ask you so many questions." And also make sure Bragi woke up, but I wasn't willing to admit that.

"But?" Maeve prompted.

"But Nico, the man the salve is for, he's waiting for me." He was probably safe, but he was also probably worried.

"I can't have another magical being here. It's hard enough to keep my magics in place with you and Bragi, especially with you leaking power the way you are."

I was doing what? "I'm not."

"You are. A conduit can only have so much flow through them at once."

A what now? "A conduit? Me?"

"You didn't know." She tilted her head and studied me.

What did she see that I couldn't? "I don't even know what that means."

"I can only tell you the basics, because they're rare. You'd have to find someone with more experience to give you the full story. But it's exactly what it sounds like. Power can flow through you, and right now, it's not only leaking out, but it's disrupting other magic, because of it."

I felt like that explained so much, and at the same time, absolutely nothing. Was that why my shields had failed when we went to Nico's? "I don't suppose... Do you know any way to, I don't know, turn off the spigot?"

"Give me a minute." Maeve stood and walked from the room.

A minute turned into two, and then five, based on the counting in my brain that I couldn't stop. Should I follow her? Was there a problem?

"Here it is." She returned right as I was about to go looking, stepped behind me, and hooked something around my neck.

The instant the necklace touched my skin, an odd sense of comfort wrapped around me. It didn't silence my concern or quiet my anxiety, but it made me feel better.

I lifted the crystal pendant attached to a soft leather cord. "What is it?"

"Only temporary, based on how powerful you are. It will catch and dissipate a bit of what's spilling from you. You'll need to find someone who can give you a more permanent fix."

"Like what?" I was still trying to wrap my brain around this download of massive information.

"Some sort of mark meant to help control power. It's not a difficult magic, and if it's done right it works a bit like a spigot, but it does need to come from someone who's practiced. Also, once you've had the children, you won't be like this all the time."

So she did know. Wait. "I'm accessing their power?" Fuck. "Is that why I can feel what other people are feeling?"

Maeve raised her brows. "Are they Bragi's?"

"One of them. He doesn't know. Please..."

"It's not my place to say." Maeve moved into the kitchen, and filled a kettle with water. "Let's have that tea. If your friend is okay, call him. Tell him you are as well, and then stay."

Such a simple plan. I had no illusions that life would stay easy, but I was going to take advantage of this calm, even if it only meant five more minutes of it, and especially if it meant learning about my mothers.

CHAPTER 13

BRAGI

I felt like death worked over.

But I was alive.

I also seemed to be in a strange bed, and shirtless.

Maeve's. That was where I was. Magnus had shown up. I didn't remember much after that, but what kind of an ass was I, that I couldn't defend myself?

I assumed Maeve hadn't been happy about the fighting on her border, and had stepped in. She'd saved me.

What did she do to Magnus? The thought took far too long to penetrate my pain-addled brain. I needed to know that Magnus was all right.

Dizziness threatened to engulf me as I pushed to my feet, and I ignored it. As long as I could stand—speak—I needed answers.

The longer I was conscious, the more my surroundings sank in, and I followed the sounds coming from the other room.

Was that laughter?

The cabin layout was familiar, but the decor had changed since I was last here. The retro-modern had been replaced with something more earthy and classic.

I found Magnus in the kitchen with Maeve, the two of them laughing at something.

I didn't get to see Magnus like this very often—with a carefree smile and that gleam in her emerald-green eyes.

Fuck she was gorgeous.

"Morning, Sleeping Beauty." Maeve greeted me when she saw me.

Magnus gave me her attention as well, and while her smile muted, it didn't vanish. "How are you feeling?"

"Alive. I assume thanks to both of you." My backpack sat in the corner, and it appeared unopened. But I doubted half of what was in it would hold the same appeal as if I'd gotten here when it was fresh.

I had questions, but protocol had to be observed. "I offer my gratitude, Maeve." She hated the honorifics she'd once adored. Ever since she dared fall for a mortal and lost her throne... "And I owe you for taking care of my friend."

Maeve shook her head. "Magnus has paid her own debt."

What did that mean? I'd ask, but I wouldn't get an answer. This was where having my empathy would come in handy. Except, not with Maeve. I'd never been able to read her.

"You should sit." Magnus toed an empty chair toward me, as if it were completely natural for her to invite me to make myself at home in someone else's house.

Things were definitely amiss here. While Maeve didn't care for formality, she observed it because expectations had to be met. *Let people see you slip once, and they'll think it's the new status quo.*

Maeve nodded at the same seat. "Join us. Tell me why you're here. Let's get the business out of the way."

That was more like it. I grabbed my bag and took a seat. "I'd like to ask you to make me a sticky salve."

Maeve clucked. "You're trying it again."

"It's for a friend." I expected her to say this wouldn't be cheap. It never was. I opened the bag, and frowned when I saw most of the contents were squashed. "My gifts didn't make it. I will bring replacements."

Maeve shrugged. "Let's see anyway. Unless it's inedible, I might make an exception. If you swear to not speak of this to anyone."

Who was I dealing with and what had Magnus given her?

I extracted a large, bottled Coke—the one item that was still intact—and set it in front of Maeve. A cinnamon roll that was more of a pancake. And the sauce and bread-pate filled package from the pizza place she loved in a nearby town. It had held a calzone. Now, it was nothing more than a mess.

These were all things she could get on her own, but it was the gifting and the consideration that mattered.

Maeve grabbed the drink and flicked the lid with her thumb. The cap popped off with a soft *hiss* and clattered against the tabletop, spinning to a stop. "You were always my favorite." She took a long drink.

She said that to anyone who brought her the right food.

I had no issue with that. "What else do you need? Finishing ingredients."

"What's it for? What has your friend lost?"

Magnus was quiet, as she had been since I walked in the room. Her expression was contemplative.

I would've expected at least one snarky comment from her by now. How was I going to get her to forgive me if I couldn't tell what she was feeling?

"I need two." I was taking a risk asking for more, but if there was ever a time to push my luck, this felt like it. "One for memories, and one for magical energy."

Maeve raised her brows.

Magnus cleared her throat with a loud cough. "*It's for a friend*," she mimicked my earlier statement.

There it was. At least that was what I expected. I shrugged. "I'm here. I have to ask."

"I'll do it, because I like Magnus," Maeve said. "But the requirements are complicated." She rattled off a list of items, and I committed them to memory. She wouldn't repeat herself.

"Something to do. Finally." Magnus let out a tiny exhale that sounded a lot like relief.

It must be gnawing at her to not have a way to take action. "I'm not sure this is what you're looking for. Most of this can be found in markets."

"Like we hop down to the Piggly Wiggly?" Magnus asked.

Maeve stared at her, blinking rapidly a few times. "Beg pardon. The what?"

Magnus smirked. "It's a grocery store. Down south. You don't get out much, do you?"

"Not a lot of call for it."

"When this is done, I'll introduce you to Dahlia and we'll take you shopping." Magnus's enthusiasm trailed off to nothing by the end of the sentence.

Maeve nodded. "When this is done. Yes."

I was sorry I'd slept through whatever tran-spired between them. "To answer your question, no.

More like street vendors." I ticked through the mental list, as much to cement it in my head as to assign buying locations. "France. Qatar. Fiji. Etcetera."

"It's still taking action," Magnus said.

"And you can replace your payment when you return, Bragi." Maeve finished off the soda.

Magnus stood. "Thank you. For everything. We should get back to Nico." She wobbled on her feet and steadied herself with the back of her chair.

Maeve was on her feet as quickly as I was, both of us moving to Magnus's side.

That was odd.

"Are you all right?" I asked.

Magnus pulled away from us. "Fine. Really. I feel bad about leaving him alone for so long."

"You called him, and he told you he was fine." Maeve tilted her head and studied Magnus. "When was the last time you slept?"

"Last night?" Magnus's reply was less than convincing.

Maeve sighed. "*Actually* slept."

"2015? I don't know. I'll be fine."

"Yes. You will be." Maeve brushed her fingers along Magnus's forehead, and Magnus wobbled.

I caught her before she hit the ground, and lifted her unconscious—sleeping?—form. "You could've hurt her."

"I knew you had her." Maeve returned to her

seat. "Put her in my bed. I suspect the one you were in needs clean sheets."

"No. Really. What happened while I was out?" None of her behavior made sense to me.

Maeve picked at the squashed calzone with a frown. "Girl talk. She'll sleep for a while—she needs it—and you and I need to talk."

I didn't have an argument. In Maeve's room I tucked Magnus in, then returned to the kitchen.

"Your friend stopped by a few weeks ago," Maeve said as I took my seat again.

Simple phrase. It could mean a lot of things, but it was specific, and the information made my blood run cold. Vidar had been here. "I don't suppose you're willing to say why."

"He was looking for the smoky quartz crystal that's currently hanging around Magnus's neck. Rather, he was looking for that on a much larger scale."

I'd noticed the jewelry, and assumed it was just another accessory Magnus decided to wear. I should've looked closer. Known better. "You gave that to her."

"I did."

Whatever bond had formed between Magnus and Maeve, whatever connected them, I needed it to be strong enough for Maeve to give me real answers. "Vidar wants something from her, and we don't know what."

Maeve dipped her head with a frown, and her entire body heaved with her sigh. "I told her this, but it seems you need to know too. She's a conduit."

Fuck. How long had Vidar known? Dahlia wasn't his end game—which was why he was willing to let her go, when she and Magnus left TOM. Why he worked so hard to keep Magnus there. To get closer to her.

That had to be his reason.

Because for a being who always wanted *more*, having control of something—someone—that would siphon that power directly into him was an ultimate goal.

Maeve met my gaze. "You have to keep him away from her."

"I will." I didn't know how, but if it meant burning everything to prevent Vidar from using Magnus, that was what I would do.

CHAPTER 14

NICODEMUS

The way Magnus hurried out of here was a stark contrast to the cheer in her voice when she'd called a few hours ago. *"This is going to take a while,"* she said. *"We're both fine, or I am and Bragi will be. I'm sorry to leave you alone for so long. I'm sorry for so much of this."*

I assured her this was the best time I'd had since I *woke up*. That was what it was becoming in my mind—the day I woke up with no memories.

I could see why I'd been drawn to her before. To both of them. It was also clear to me how intense the attraction was between them, despite how hard they fought it.

Since I had nothing to do but wait, I'd grabbed the book we'd borrowed from Gwydion, and began to read. It was a collection of old fairytales. Though, not so old I would've heard them when I was a child.

It was difficult to wrap my brain around being so old. How many centuries had I seen come and go? Did I appreciate as the culture changed? The technology? Was I aware when cars were invented? Indoor plumbing? The number one?

Too many questions without answers, so I lost myself in children's tales instead. There was one about a witch who kidnapped a woman's husband, and because she couldn't have him, she trapped him in a dream.

There was another about a great wolf who attacked a woman. Fate and the gods intervened, deciding death wouldn't be her final fate.

So many stories. About bears who fought great battles, and artists who could breathe magic into a person with their ink. Humans who became fae, and a woman who could amplify the strength of those around her, and gates and keys and crystals and a magical spring.

It was all fantastic. How much of it was real and how much was whimsy?

When my phone rang, I was surprised. Was Magnus going to be even later? "Hello," I answered.

"Nico." It was Bragi. "Is all well?"

"A little dull without an immediate threat, but otherwise, yes." I kept my tone light, to let him know I was teasing.

He huffed a laugh. "I wanted to let you know this

is taking longer than expected. However, we will be back in a few hours."

I was surprised to be hearing from him, given Magnus said he needed to recover. "Is everything all right?"

"It is. And I have one hel of a story to tell when we return." He sounded lighter than he had since I met him.

"I look forward to it."

"Nico." Bragi's voice caught me as I was going to hang up. "In my suitcase, there's a stack of notebooks. Journals from when I knew you. They may not make sense, you may not be able to read my chicken scratch, but you're welcome to read them."

That sounded personal. Far more so than listening to a dictated tale. "Thank you. I'll see you both when you return."

As I disconnected, conflict warred inside me. *Journals.* Such a personal thing. Did I wish to step that deeply inside his head when I couldn't even do so for myself?

It may provide insight into me, and it would definitely do so about him.

I wasn't sure I could read any more fairytales. It felt wicked opening Bragi's bag while he wasn't here, but I didn't need to dig through all his unmentionables. I found the leather bound books wrapped together with a leather cord, and tucked securely in one corner of the suitcase.

The only way to unwrap the stack, as far as I was concerned, was with reverence. I set the binding and all but one of the books on the coffee table, settled back, and opened the top book.

Letters and words were scrawled in inconsistent ink across the pages. It took a few minutes for me to decipher sentences, thanks to an older dialect, fading lines, and flowing scribbles, but once I understood the style, I found myself falling into it.

The stream of consciousness about the first time Bragi met me was intimate. The way he described me, with flowery adoration, made heat rush to my face.

As the days continued, though he and I had parted ways, some of the entries were sweet and others were analytical, but I appeared in many of them.

When I reached our second meeting, the description of how he felt about our kisses was erotic enough to scorch the paper.

I so desperately wished the emotions flowing through me were attached to my own memories of these events. Bragi was a beautiful storyteller, even talking to a blank page, but I wanted to live these intense moments from my own perspective.

I closed Book Two and set it aside. I needed a break. To get some air.

Dahlia and Magnus had explained the protections around the cabin extended quite a ways. So we wouldn't be confined to the small room. Which was good because I needed to walk.

When I stepped outside, a chill wrapped around me. Nighttime in the desert. Though the air was cold against my face and arms, it didn't penetrate. Was that me, keeping me warm?

The space here was so... *big*, and under the dark night sky it felt like I could fall in any direction and never stop. It was both terrifying and awe inspiring. I picked a direction and walked, occasionally glancing over my shoulder to make sure I could still see the light of the cabin.

The longer I was out here, the less I looked back. The walking didn't clear my head, but it did help me slot thoughts more neatly. It also left an itch in my back. My shoulders. Not the kind that one could physically scratch. It was a desire to *move*.

I *was* moving though. Walking. Enjoying. There was so much wide open space around me, and the vast expanse of open nothing whispered in my ear. My attention was drawn to the sky as much as the ground, and that feeling of falling up flitted through me. It flowed into my hands and feet, and encased me until I swore I could touch the stars.

I was barely aware of reaching for the pinpricks of light. Were they getting closer? The wind rushed hard past my face, and I looked down.

The ground was several meters below me. I was flying.

The rush of air was no longer cold, or at least it didn't feel that way, and the wind didn't tear at my bare skin. Instead, I swooped and soared, riding air currents as if I'd always done it.

Then again, I probably had.

I lost track of time, gliding flying until the black sky turned gray and the faintest hints of light peeked over the mountains in the distance.

It was probably time to get back. I was reluctant to land, but I could go out again. I could *fly*, and now I knew it. The feeling buoyed my spirits and lifted my mood.

How did I go back to my other form?

I swooped toward the ground, and as it rushed up to meet me, my human feet touched down. It took a moment to adjust to the solid ground, but I found my footing quickly.

That was incredible. "*Whoo.*" I couldn't help but let out the shout.

What else could I do that was muscle memory?

I had to figure it out.

CHAPTER 15
MAGNUS

I was in Bragi's bedroom. That wasn't...

Wasn't what? The thought flitted away before I could grasp it.

Lips pressed into my bare shoulder, sending a delicious shiver through me.

Nico.

I couldn't feel what he felt, but his touch along my naked back, his fingers drawing lightly up my spine, was delicious.

In front of me, Bragi tilted my chin up and claimed my mouth with his, in a hard, hungry kiss.

I leaned into the sensation, wanting more. *Needing* more.

This isn't right.

This was incredible. Trapped between them, none of us clothed, and all of our hands and mouths roaming everywhere. Heat swelled inside me, pooling in my belly and traveling lower to pulse between my thighs.

He's lying.

Who? Bragi. He wasn't, though. He wanted me.

This ends badly.

This would end in orgasms. They were both worshiping me with their touch. He wanted to keep me safe.

No.

The thought was a barely whispered word that drifted away before I could figure out what it meant. I wanted it to come back. To explain. Knowing what I was trying to tell myself was more important than being with them.

What was wrong with me? Why couldn't I just enjoy this?

The dream was gone, and my eyes flew open without my permission. I was in a bedroom I didn't recognize, and Bragi had his back to me, as he left the room.

I wanted him. Intensely. Desperately. To taste him. To hear intimately filthy words spill from his lips and caress my ears. To feel him buried inside me.

No. He'd lied to me. He let me think Dahlia was dead. He told me my entire world was gone, so he could keep me in his.

So he could keep me safe. The same way I'm pushing Dahlia away to keep her safe.

The two were *not* the same. I wasn't taking Dahlia's freedom.

And speaking of Dahlia, I only had that stupid dream because watching her play kissy-face with two sexy gods made me lonely. Horny.

It had nothing to do with me still wanting Bragi. Because I didn't.

Or maybe just a little.

I adjusted myself in the bed, and he paused and turned.

"You're awake," he said. No feelings radiated from him, at least not anything identifiable. It was more like the faintest hint of sugar in the air the day after baking cookies, rather than reminding me of walking by a perfume counter.

This crystal from Maeve was amazing. "Yeah."

"Are you all right?" He stayed at the edge of the room. "You were whimpering in your sleep."

Fuck. I didn't moan his name or anything, did I? "I probably do that most of the time." I could brush it off as a nightmare. Technically it was, wasn't it?

"I remember."

A simple response, but it tied to an avalanche of the past. He shouldn't remember. He never should've been there while I slept. While I healed. Even though he helped me. He healed me. He shouldn't have been a part of that. Wouldn't have been, if he told me the truth.

He was just like Johnny.

Not quite.

Fuck me and my needy, clingy, sex-deprived brain. "You could've woken me up if I was having bad dreams." Would that have been better or worse? To have him hovering over me while I was dreaming about how much I enjoyed fucking him?

"It won't stop you from having them, and if I let you sleep, maybe this time you wouldn't remember when you woke up. Besides, you needed the rest."

That last bit was probably true. I hated to admit it, but I felt rested. I also felt like an asshole for falling asleep in the middle of what was technically a mission. Why had I...? That wasn't like me. "I'm sorry for passing out."

"It wasn't your fault. Literally. Maeve put you to sleep."

I wasn't sure I liked that.

Bragi closed the door and approached me, stopping a meter or so from the bed. "May we talk?"

No. "We are talking."

"Fair." His smile was dry. "I realize I don't have any right to ask, but I'm going to anyway. I need a favor. I need your help."

"You're right. You don't deserve to ask." I pushed myself into a sitting position in the bed. Thankfully I was fully clothed, aside from my shoes, which I took off myself, earlier. I nodded at the foot of the mattress. "What is it?"

He didn't sit. "What I did to you, to get your

Valkyrie powers back... I'd like you to do the same to me."

Right. The torture. The agony. The hours of sitting through having magical bones broken, so I could be whole again. Gwydion had looked disgusted that Bragi knew such a thing. I should be jumping at the chance to make him suffer.

"I can't." The idea of inflicting that kind of pain on anyone besides Vidar made my gut churn. "Even if I wanted to, I don't know how. That's like asking someone who's had open heart surgery to perform it themselves."

"It's not like that at all," Bragi said. "I can walk you through it. You understand the concept, and I think you can do it."

But I couldn't. "I'm sorry."

Bragi pursed his lips and gave a terse nod. He sat at the end of the bed, still keeping space between us. "Why are you doing this for Nico?" He asked. "You knew him for a month."

This was less than subtle. How would he twist my words to get the answers from me that he wanted?

But will he?

"Because he needs my help." Sure, my response could be easily turned on me. Bragi could counter *so do I*. Was I testing him? Was I asking to be convinced?

"Or is it because he was good to you when you were broken? Comforted you when you thought you'd lost it all, and showed you the light in a world that's always been a dark and bitter place for you. That's not love, you know."

Bragi's words tugged at my innermost insecurities. Barely a nudge, but enough to remind me the doubts were there.

I couldn't lay here anymore. This conversation made me itch to move, because it was a reminder we were wasting time. I climbed from the bed so I could work off some of the tension pumping in my legs.

"I *do* know that's not love." Joke was on him. I'd spent the last month torturing myself with similar questions—*why is it so important to me that Nico remembers?* "But it could be. Maybe I just have the feeling he and I are meant to be together." That was true, but it was also me throwing Bragi's approach to us back in his face.

His raised eyebrows made me think he didn't appreciate the jab. "Let's say that's the only reason. What's your plan? Play house until he falls again?"

"You know the plan." Albeit, it wasn't much of one. "We follow every path that might have answers until we find the one that restores him."

Bragi grabbed my hand, yanking me to a stop. He met my gaze and held it. "First of all, that's not a plan, it's a prayer, and we both know those don't work. Second, you're trying oh so hard to not answer the original question. Why is *this,* why is Nico recovering his memory so important to *you?*"

The longer Bragi held on, the more want built inside me, drawing up the dream. The good parts of our time together. "Because he saved me." The answer slipped out without my permission, thanks to the mental onslaught. "And if he falls for me in the process of rediscovering who he is, if I fall for him, then that's not bad either."

I didn't want to admit any of that, not even to myself. But there it was.

"That's not the only reason," Bragi said.

Fuck him for trying to climb inside my head and for being desirable and for making my body want him even when my head knew better. "It is as far as you're concerned." I still couldn't make myself pull away from his grip.

I was stronger than that. Could control who I was. I yanked free and spun away.

Bragi stepped in my path, and I pulled up short, my breath catching at how close he stood. How imposing he could be when he wanted to.

"Tell me." His tone was pure command. "Why?"

"Because you—Vidar, Hel, all of you at TOM— told us we could save the world." Once upon a time, I believed that they believed that bullshit. "You all lied. The only reason you recruited us was to do your dirty work. To save *your* world."

Bragi winced.

Good.

Now that I was talking, I had to finish. "Kirby made me a Valkyrie. That should've been what I needed—finally enough power to make a difference. No." Bitterness bled into my voice and I didn't try to stop it. "Everyone around me still suffers. I can't stop Vidar. Hell, I almost caved to Minato, and I would've without Dahlia. I was supposed to be a hero. I was supposed to make the world a better place. And now you're asking for the same thing again. *Help me get my power back. Make me a god again. Make my dick work so I can fuck the world some more.*"

Bragi's eyes narrowed. "You think I want this for me. I don't."

"Bullshit." I knew better. "If you say it's to protect me—to save Nico—I still call bullshit, because I never asked you to save me, and that's still you being selfish."

"None of us are heroes." Bragi's words dug deep.

"Speak for yourself."

"I am. I'm speaking for me and for every person you know and love. Did you think you'd be Luke Skywalker, following an implausible path of making every single right decision and only having to watch bad people die? Do you think you're Steve Rogers? Because he did everything right, and he still had days where he didn't win."

I needed to step back. Put some distance between us so I could think. "Don't mock me."

"I'm not." Bragi's voice was hard. "You keep asking for honesty—this is it. Would you rather I use more personal examples? Is Kirby your bar? Your real life Supergirl? She's not a lawful good paladin. She broke the rules when she defied Odin, and she wasn't thinking about the cost anyone would pay, as long as Starkad survived. Are you looking at Dahlia? As I said to her, she'd let everyone else burn to save you and her men."

Dahlia was good and kind and sweet and generous. "No she wouldn't." I refused to concede Bragi's point, even if it was a good one.

"She would," he said. "If it came down to it, if there were no other choice... You can't save everyone. No one can. I lo—"

"Don't you dare." I refused to hear *I love you for trying* from his mouth.

"You can stop me from saying it, but it won't change anything."

I raked my fingers through my hair and yanked hard on the strands. "I know I can't save the world, but I have to be able to save *someone*. Nico gave me my life. Twice. If I can't fucking save just one person who deserves it..." I was useless.

Bragi grabbed my wrist again, and pulled my hand from my head before I could rip out my hair.

His grip was softer this time. Powerful but gentle. How was that possible?

"I don't expect you to like my words," he said. "And I'm not trying to change your mind. I *know* your perspective is different from theirs. From all of ours. When you say you want to save people, I believe you."

He dragged in a deep breath. "Your friends—they want security. They want to belong. They want vengeance. If you think that's not what drives Kirby, you're lying to yourself. I don't have a problem with their motivation, but it's not yours. You want justice and equity and for everyone good to have everything good."

I hated that his words warmed me, and that he could see so deep inside me. I hated the adoration and that I wanted to bask in it.

"That's why I stopped doing what I was doing, with TOM," Bragi said. "Because I saw that in you, and..." He let out a long sigh and moved his hand from my arm to my face.

His touch was so light, my breath caught. He traced a thumb along my cheek. Light. Barely there. Seductive and mournful.

I couldn't grasp the fight inside. The voice that wanted me to pull away was so quiet. It would be easy to fall into this. Into Bragi and his touch. Into the way he saw me.

He dipped his head and hovered his mouth over

mine. His breath was heated temptation teasing my lips.

"I *do* want my powers back for me," he whispered. "It's selfish, and I don't deny that. I want my strength back so I can keep you safe. Even if you think you don't need me, you can't face the world alone. No one should have to even try. And I refuse to let Vidar or anyone remove you or what you are from this existence."

Though the hard edge was gone from his voice, the conviction was stronger than ever. The intensity in his gaze, in his words, wrapped around me. I wanted him to kiss me. I wanted to lean in and feel him and taste him.

I knew better.

I forced myself to step away and break the contact between us. The desire to tell him *no* was gone, though. Used up in this single moment. "Okay. I'll help you. I'll see if I can restore your power."

"While we're here, safe and isolated, I'd just like to see if you can do it. I expect it will take multiple iterations, as it did with you." Bragi's voice was thick, as he jerked his head toward the middle of the room.

Did the exchange between us impact him as much as it did me?

I already knew the answer was *yes*. "It's going to hurt." Way to state the obvious, me. Still, he deserved a reminder. Anyone did before willingly walking into this.

"I know." Bragi knelt on the ground, his back ramrod straight. "Once upon a time, I did it to myself. The mind numbs the pain of the past, so right now I can convince myself I can handle it."

Those were wise words. "Is that a good thing or a bad thing?"

"You tell me."

I didn't know, so my response was to kneel behind him. "This is easier if you can relax."

His entire body sagged, and some of his joints unlocked, but tension still coiled through his body. Easy enough to spot after a lifetime of needing to be aware of it in myself and others.

"That's as good as it gets," Bragi said.

Fair enough.

From what he'd told me before, skin-to-skin contact made this process more effective, so I wasn't surprised to see him unbutton his shirt and slide it halfway down his back, leaving his shoulders and scars exposed.

What kind of magic did it take to leave that many marks on a man who was immortal?

I reached for him and stopped. What if touching him was like when I kissed Nico? The crystal was keeping me from feeling his emotions, but...

I shook the hesitation aside. There hadn't been anyone but me in my heart when he grabbed me before. I should be fine. Aside from one other tiny issue.

"Is there a problem?" Bragi asked.

"I understand in theory what you did, but going back to the heart surgeon analogy, I don't know how."

"Look for the threads that run through me. They'll be faint, like a series of glowing threads."

Sounded simple enough. "I can't see anything." Did that mean I was the problem, or his magic was that far gone?

"Are you sure?"

Why was he questioning me? "Why are you so sure I should be able to?"

"I can't help but watch you." Bragi glanced over his shoulder. "And I know what it's like to have the emotions of every nearby person spilling through me. The last few days, until we got here, the way you've been reacting..."

So much for hiding what I was feeling.

"I don't know if what you're experiencing came from me or not," he said. "But if it did, it stands to reason you can do other things that I could, as well. Focus."

Easy for him to say. "I can't see anything."

"You may have to take the crystal off."

If it was keeping me from feeling him, it made sense that it would keep me from doing other things, too. I wasn't sure I was ready for this.

He turned away as I slipped the necklace off. "I'm sorry," his voice was soft.

There he was. His every feeling mingling with mine.

"You can push it into the background if you focus." Bragi's voice cut through the emotional noise.

I'd heard that so many times in school. *Just block out what you feel. Focus on anything else.* Was it better or worse that he'd taught us based on his personal experiences?

Was I actually grateful I knew how to do this? It was difficult to claw through all the feelings, to find my way to a place where I *could* focus. The last thing I wanted was to lose myself in the intensity of his emotions—mine were bad enough.

Thankfully, Bragi didn't say a word, and I suspected he was working to keep himself from feeling.

How did he do this for eons and not go insane?

It took me a few minutes, but I managed to wrap up what I felt from Bragi, and shove it into the same box in the back of my mind where I kept my own distractions.

"Okay." I breathed out the confirmation.

"Good. Now concentrate on what you can see. Study my back. Can you see the threads?"

No.

But I could. The faintest crisscross of silver lines

running under and through his skin. Hundreds. Thousands. How was I supposed to keep track of them all?

"You only need to pick one," Bragi spoke in a low, tightly controlled tone.

How? I reached, and was surprised when I made contact with a cord at the edge of the maze.

I expected to pluck, and the connection would sever. It took more than that. I felt the resistance from the magical cord. Felt the crack in my fingers when it snapped. Felt Bragi's agony, despite him barely grunting.

How many more times did I have to do this?

Something surged in my head. A feeling that amplified the world. Everything rushed in at once. The sounds. The ambient magic in the air. The—

"What the fuck are you doing?" The door slammed open and Maeve stalked in. She crossed the room in a blink, grabbed the necklace from where it lay on the ground, and handed it to me.

As she pressed the crystal tightly into my palm, the onslaught subsided, and I was me again. I slipped the cord around my neck without hesitation. Sweet, sweet silence blanketed my mind.

Maeve fixed an angry glare on Bragi, who climbed to his feet as he pulled his shirt on.

"I can't believe you asked this of her." Maeve spoke through clenched teeth. "And you." She whirled on me, beautiful and terrifying. "I don't know if you have a death wish, but I assume you want to see your children survive."

Well, fuck.

Bragi's eyes grew wide.

"You cannot do this. You risk not only your life, but your children's," she said.

"Children?" Bragi repeated.

CHAPTER 16

BRAGI

Magnus's children.

Plural.

"You're pregnant." I stared at her in disbelief as my mind caught up to what Maeve had just said. "Twins." Both mine? At least one because as a conduit, that was how she was able to channel power like mine.

Magnus was carrying my children.

Holy shit.

She refused to look at me.

Maeve stepped between Magnus and me, rage splashed across her face. I forced myself to give her my attention.

"It's true that most of what I do is about the ritual." Maeve looked like the edge of a furious storm. Looming and ready to erupt at any moment. "I ask for tiny things. Insignificant in the grand scheme of the universe. I only ask for one or two small courtesies in return. For instance, not using magic in my realm. *Especially* not this abomination of a technique that you swore to me would only be used on you by you."

Maeve clenched her fists. "And now I come in here to find that you've not only coerced someone else into using it, you've used it on her in the past."

"I did what I had to. I only apologize for doing it here." The only thing I'd do differently, if faced with the decision again, would be to wait until Magnus and I had left.

Though I may not. Having her here, for Maeve to attend to when it went wrong, had been the right decision.

"Not good enough." Maeve bit off the words. "In response to your request, your reason for being here, the answer is *no*. I will not make the salve. Not for you and not for your friend."

Fuck. I deserved punishment, but Nico didn't. "You—"

"But—"

Maeve held up her index finger, silencing both Magnus and me, and fixed me with a glare. "Don't move."

Maeve turned to Magnus.

I struggled against the invisible bonds Maeve used to lock me in place. I fought the restraints for all I was worth. She couldn't hurt Magnus. I wouldn't let her. The last few hours, while Magnus slept, Maeve said fewer than five words to me. I had no idea what the two of the had talked about while I was recovering, but if I'd just undone it, if I'd just cost Magnus anything—

"I'll make the unguent for you," Maeve said to Magnus. "For your friend. And you will owe me."

"I will. Please and thank you." Magnus's voice was submissive. "Whatever you want."

"I'd say it's a simple request, but you two have proven we don't define that the same way. Keep the children safe. That includes coming back to me for care, or someone else you trust implicitly."

Joke was on her. Magnus didn't trust anyone who had that kind of knowledge.

"All right." Magnus's answer was immediate.

"Swear to me. Give me your word that I will never see him again." Maeve jerked her head in my direction.

Magnus hesitated. It was only for a single breath, but it was enough. "I give you my word," she conceded.

There were worse punishments.

"Good." Maeve wiggled her fingers, and I could move again. "Magnus, when you have the remaining ingredients, you may return here. Alone. Until then, both of you go home."

We were no longer in Maeve's cabin. Instead we stood at the edge of Dahlia's wards. The instant our feet hit the ground, Magnus stepped toward the cabin, and I followed, putting us inside the safe zone.

"I had to promise her," Magnus said as she walked.

"I don't blame you." I kept pace, and kept an eye on our surroundings. Knowing we were inside a protective bubble didn't erase this feeling of being out in the open, exposed. Especially because we were being hunted by a man who had trained snipers and witches and demigods at his beck and call. "I apologize that my actions directed any of her wrath at you."

Magnus strode with purpose, attention flitting like mine, and path straight. "She knew my mothers. Did you know that?"

What? "No. I swear to you, I would've told you."

"Uh-huh. She delivered me. She was there when I was born."

That explained the bond between them. I wanted to focus on this news that Maeve had information about where Magnus came from, but for me, something else was far more important. "Speaking of… You're pregnant."

Her footsteps faltered, but only for an instant. "I won't talk to you about this."

"How long have you known?"

"Not talking about it."

"Are they both mine?"

"Neither one is yours."

That wasn't going to cut it with me. "Bullshit. Your empathy and ability to see certain kinds of magic didn't come from nowhere overnight. At least one of them is mine. I know someone who excels at prenatal care for gods. He can—"

"No." Magnus clipped the word. "You don't have a say in this pregnancy. You won't be involved with it. You won't be a part of their lives when they're born."

Like Hel I wouldn't. "At least one of them is mine." I was becoming a broken record, but I would push until she admitted it. I knew exactly what a conduit was, because Vidar had been searching for one for nearly a century. Apparently he'd found one, in Magnus.

Magnus stared me down with a gaze that might burn a hole in my soul if I looked long enough. "Both of them are mine. One might carry your power, and the other Nico's, but fate gave them to me, not you."

I could argue that I couldn't be the one who was pregnant, but gods and childbirth were chaotic. I very well could be. Conceding her point meant surrendering.

Pushing her meant she'd shut me out even more.

I'd drop the discussion for now, but it wasn't over.

She waited, as if expecting me to say something, and when I didn't, she started walking again.

A short while later, we reached the cabin. When we entered, Nico was asleep on the futon.

I hoped he didn't stay up all night waiting for us, though I knew him well enough to recognize he probably had done exactly that.

"I need food," Magnus muttered, and cut a wide path around me to get into the kitchen. She set the coffee to brew, and poured herself a massive bowl of chocolate something.

"You should have something more substantial than Cocoa Puffs and a mocha, given your condition." I knew the instant I said the words that they were a mistake, even without her glare.

"And what would be appropriate given *your* condition? Monster energy drink? Give you a little extra pep to make up for what you're missing?"

I hated that she thought I was a monster. I had been, for decades, but I wanted her to see—

"What condition?" Nico's voice came from behind me.

A low rumble, like a cat growling to warn off unwanted advances, rolled from Magnus's chest, and she faced both of us. "Let's get this over with. I'm pregnant," she said. "Twins. Bragi is the father of one, and Nico, you're the father of the other. I haven't known for long. I didn't tell either of you because I didn't want Bragi to know, and I didn't want Nico to feel obligated to a woman and children he didn't know. Questions?"

So very many. All of them would wait, because Magnus's safety was a priority now more than ever. "Magnus, you're going back to NEON," I said. "Take Nico if you want, if he wants, but you're going to plant yourself behind the thickest, heaviest, safest magical walls you can find." If I couldn't keep her safe, she needed to be somewhere that they could.

Magnus stared me down as she shoved a giant spoonful of cereal into her mouth.

I assumed that was her way of saying *no*. "You and Dahlia are always strongest together."

Magnus shook her head.

"Why not?" Nico asked.

Because she was stubborn and strong-willed and that was what made her incredible. In moments like this, I also hated it. "Because Vidar threatened her."

"You don't... No." Magnus mumbled through her food.

"It's what he does." And it was time to stop pretending I didn't recognize it. "He gives you a choice. He makes you pick. He told Magnus she could pick between Dahlia and her children, and Magnus thinks she can pick both."

"I can." She pushed her food aside with a scowl.

If anyone could, it was her. Except that she was making a massive mistake.

"Not as long as you're being an idiot about it." I didn't like the language, but they got my point across. "If you keep doing what he wants you to—

avoiding Dahlia—he gets his way." I reached across the counter and grabbed Magnus's purse before she could stop me. I plucked out her phone and handed it to her. "Call Dahlia. Go someplace safe."

"Go. Fuck. Yourself." Magnus took the device and jammed it into her pocket.

She was making decisions because I didn't want her to. Fuck. "Don't do this to spite me. There's no point in that."

"I don't do anything because you said to do so or not to do so," Magnus said. "I'm not a child throwing a tantrum. But every time you push, I have to ask myself why. Every time you insist something is best for me, I have to step back and wonder what's in it for you. Even something as simple as going where I should be safe. What do you get out of it?"

"I get you being safe." I couldn't make it any clearer.

I also understood why she didn't trust me, and I didn't know how to fix that.

CHAPTER 17

NICODEMUS

I didn't mean to fall asleep. I had so much I wanted to tell Magnus and Bragi about. The attack. The flying. That I could use my powers.

Somehow, they managed to come back with news at least as important as that.

Magnus was pregnant.

One of the babies was mine.

Vidar knew it and had threatened her.

Because somehow that would make her super powerful when she was with Dahlia.

The glow around Magnus—which I understood now was an aura—was distorted and fuzzy, compared to when she left.

And perhaps there was a trick in Bragi wanting to keep Magnus safe? I didn't understand what it would be, but I also didn't blame Magnus for being cautious.

This was moving too fast. We had too much information and not enough answers. "We need to slow down and put some pieces together."

"We need to stop talking and act," Magnus countered. "We've already wasted so much time. Nico's memories... Vidar... We don't know what to do about any of it."

"*You* need to be somewhere safe." Bragi was holding firm, too. "I've already lost you both once. And it was my fault. I'm not making that mistake again."

"Instead you'll make whole new ones," Magnus said.

Bragi scowled. "You're the one pursuing an avenue that won't work."

I wasn't going to watch them argue in circles again. "*Stop.*"

They both gave me their attention at the sharp bark, but neither looked happy about it.

"Magnus, are we currently safe, at least for an hour or two?" I asked.

She worked her jaw. "There are no guarantees, but otherwise, yes."

"Then we have at least a little time to think." It felt like a reasonable request to me.

"And then overthink, and overcomplicate, and then Vidar's there again, waiting and ready for our next fuck-up, and you won't be safe, Nico, and Dahlia will be in danger, and—" Magnus furrowed her brow and snapped her jaw shut. "I'm so tired of this." She leaned against the counter behind her, and her body sagged.

"Nico's right." The way Bragi relaxed looked mechanical and unnatural. "We need to slow down, and stop reacting."

"And let Vidar continue to be one step ahead. Or more," Magnus said.

Bragi shook his head. "No. And stop doing exactly what he wants us to. He knows we care. He knows each of us has something we'll react emotionally to. It's how he got me to—"

"Hold me hostage?" Magnus finished his sentence.

"Keep you safe," Bragi corrected her.

I swallowed a comment about the difference in language. "What's one thing he doesn't want? Do we know that?"

"To be powerless." Magnus had an instant answer.

"To lose track of Magnus," Bragi said. "He doesn't want that."

I didn't blame him, but I suspected his reasons were different than mine. "Why not?"

Magnus scrubbed her face and pushed away from the counter. "I'm a conduit. I didn't know until a few hours ago, but it makes sense, doesn't it? If power flows through me, it could come from Dahlia, or it could go into him, or both."

She was a threat when she was working against him or his biggest asset if he could claim her. "And that's why he won't kill you, but why he's also working so hard to isolate you."

"Or make sure she's stuck with people who don't have any power." Bragi's retort was dry.

"I do." I held out my hand and a flame appeared in my palm.

Magnus gasped and approached me. "Do you remember?"

"No. Not technically. The muscle memory is there, though." I flicked my wrist and the fire vanished. "When I just let myself react, I can do things."

Magnus took one step away, and then another, moving closer to the door. "If he hasn't killed me yet, it means he thinks he can still use me. It means the possibility of me working with Dahlia is worth the risk of keeping me alive."

"We'll figure it out." I approached her.

She put more distance between us. "I need to think."

"Stop," Bragi warned.

"I'm not running away. We already agreed we were safe here for at least a little while." She reached the door and rested her hand on the knob. "I need some air."

Bragi started after her and I grabbed him. "The last thing she needs is your voice in her head."

"I know. She was right about one thing, though." He sighed and faced me.

She was right about all of it as far as I could tell. "What's that?"

"This approach of *doing nothing* is maddening." Bragi moved into the living room, but didn't sit. "I'm glad you're rediscovering your power. You always loved flying."

"Turns out I still do."

There were other things to talk about, but an awkward silence settled between us instead. My mind kept going back to *Magnus is pregnant. One of them is mine.*

Did I have any children anywhere else? I assumed they were more than adults. Ancient by now. What about other family?

There were so many unanswered questions.

I wanted to give Magnus all the time in the world to process, and I still believed that taking our time to think through this was the right decision, but there was a balance to be struck. After nearly an hour, I couldn't sit around anymore. "I'm going after her."

"*Thank Creation.*" Bragi's reply was a muttered huff. "Better you than me." He spoke more clearly this time, and the hint of bitterness was distinct in his voice.

I wouldn't drag her back here if she wasn't ready, but I could be a sounding board if she needed to talk things through.

I headed outside and paused. Which direction should I go? It was tempting to fly, but I didn't want to wander beyond the wards by mistake again.

"I'm over here." Magnus's call from the small grove of trees drew my attention, and I followed her voice. "I'm surprised it took one of you so long to come after me," she said when I got closer.

I looked up to see her sitting on the lower branches of one of the trees.

Though, *tree* was a generous description. They were knotted objects with sparse amounts of green, lurching from the ground amid dry patches of grass. She'd found the single tree with a perfect branch to keep her about three meters off the ground.

I leaned against the trunk and looked up at her. "Waiting seemed reasonable."

"Thank you." Magnus kicked her feet in a lazy path. "I'm sorry I dragged you into all of this."

From what I understood, she hadn't—Bragi did. "I agreed to come with you, and I suspect it was the same before, when you needed my help. That I've always been a willing participant. Besides. This is what friends do for each other, and you and we and Dahlia are stronger with each other than apart."

Magnus gave a sharp, stuttered laugh. "That sounds so cliche. So after school special."

"I don't know what that is."

"That's okay." She hopped to the ground and landed next to me on her feet. "I get your meaning and I appreciate it." She adopted a similar position to me, her shoulder resting against mine. "I can't lose Dahlia again. Or you. Or anyone who matters. And I don't know what to do, to keep that from happening."

"Every one of us is capable of deciding for ourselves if we want to be involved in this war or not, and I chose to be here. Dahlia chooses the same." I supposed it could be argued that we didn't technically choose it, but there were always points to walk away, to hide, or to just roll over and give up. "If Vidar is working this hard to keep you away from Dahlia, regardless of his reasons for letting you live, then it makes sense that being around her is a better idea than not."

"I agree," Magnus said. "And I'll call her when we go back in. I'll make sure they make room for you at NEON. Can I share a memory with you? It's not epic and sweeping, but it's about you and me, so if you're interested..."

"Of course I am." I was getting greedy when it came to these snippets of my past. "I don't care what it is, I want to hear it."

"In school they taught us sex is a tool. So is pain. That means I've used both to help me hide from the world."

I wanted to comfort her, but that didn't feel like the right response, so I stayed silent.

"When Bragi helped me get my Valkyrie powers

back, it was both intimate and agonizing. After each session, it left me craving more from him. Desperate for me to be with him."

A pit formed in my chest at the thought, leaving me conflicted. Jealous, but I also understood.

"I wanted you, too," she said softly. "There's something about you that draws me to you."

"I feel the same tug. Even after just a few days."

Her huff was part amusement, part sadness, and a third part acceptance.

Wait. Bragi had been an empath. He knew what she wanted, and that must include sex. Had he taken advantage of her? *No.* Yes?

"He wouldn't touch me." Magnus continued the story, erasing my creeping concern. "Not like that. He kept his distance after every single session, and I hated him for it."

"This is one of *my* memories?" I needed to confirm.

"It is. The first time you and I were together—the first time we fucked—was right after one of those *healing* sessions with Bragi. I was broken and lost and lonely and desperate to feel wanted. You were willing, and I used you."

That didn't sound right. Not the last bit of it, anyway. "Did I know what you wanted?"

"Yes. Rather, I told you, and you said you understood."

"Then you didn't use me."

Magnus stepped in front of me, close enough her toes touched mine, and she looked up at me through her lashes. "What if I want that from you again? The closeness and the release and all of it."

As in, what if this gorgeous, intelligent, powerful woman I hadn't been able to stop thinking about wanted to fuck me? "Then you just have to ask."

"But what if... What if I can't promise you what it means? I can't promise that it means nothing or something, but I so badly want to lose myself in you. Not someone else. *You.*"

I slid my hand to the back of her neck, and the tiniest whimper escaped her throat. The heat that flowed between us wasn't due to the sun filtering through thin branches and leaves. Touching her made me want to combust, in the best possible way.

I pressed my lips to hers, and desire surged through the connection. "Then don't promise any of those things. We don't have to know what this is beyond right now."

"Not knowing what comes next can be danger-ous." She molded her body to mine and returned the kiss. Everywhere our bodies met, embers sparked.

I couldn't stop nipping her lips. Devouring her moans. Dancing my tongue with hers and memo-rizing the way each strand wrapped around my fingers when I knotted my fingers in her hair and tugged. "It can be. But it can also be an incredible fucking ride."

Magnus draped her arms around my neck and spun us both so her back was to the tree. She pulled me closer, and I was happy to oblige.

I wanted to feel more of her. Lose myself in this greedy, demanding hunger that threatened to consume us. Part of me wanted to spend hours exploring her. Finding her buttons and giving her nothing but pleasure.

This wasn't the time or place, and the impulses that drove me insisted I get closer. Push hard. Become part of her *now*.

I roamed my mouth to her jaw and down her neck, while pushing her top up. I cupped her breasts through her bra. Each fresh gasp and sigh that escaped her lips was musical. Delicious. Hearing them all for the first time was incredible, and I hoped I'd hear them again and again.

Magnus seemed driven by a similar desperation to my own, as she dropped her hands below my waist. When she cupped my erection through my trousers, I let out a low groan, and bucked into her touch. While she stroked and teased, I undid the button and zipper on her jeans.

I slipped my hand over her panties, and damp heat beckoned me. She let out the most delicious sighs when I teased along the thin strip of fabric. I dipped near her opening, then back up, digging my fingers in when she began to grind against my touch.

How was this so intense and frantic? The entire

experience was more than physical. Whatever bound me to her, I couldn't get enough. Couldn't be close enough. I needed to be a part of Magnus.

"What is it about you?" She gasped out the question between breaths.

I wanted a similar answer about her. "It seems I have incredible taste in yummy things."

Magnus laughed. An actual, clear, bright laugh. *Creation* that sound. My new favorite.

"I don't know that I'm yummy," she said.

I dragged my tongue up her neck, to claim her mouth again. "You absolutely are delicious. Devourable."

"If you insist, who am I to argue?" As she spoke, she undid my belt and trousers. Her hot fingers wrapped around my rigid cock, and I grunted as I jerked against her touch.

No more waiting. No more teasing. "I need you now." I shoved her jeans and panties to the ground.

"*Ack.*" She giggled when her clothing got caught on her shoes. "Hang on. Hang on." She pushed the toes of one foot against the heel of the other sneaker, until she managed to kick the offending shoe off.

That was all I needed. I didn't care that her pants were still on her other leg. I lifted her, and she wrapped her arms around my shoulders and her legs around my waist. Her heat called to me. Made my cock whimper with need.

I pushed her back against the tree, and she grunted.

"Are you all right?" I hadn't picked the most comfortable surface to pin her to.

"Better than all right." Magnus's reply was breathy, and her eyes wide. "Fuck me? Please?"

There was no universe in which I could fathom telling her *no*. She worked a hand between us to guide me to her opening.

When I nudged, my desperation spiked, and when I thrust inside her, burying myself to the hilt...

"*Fuuuuuuck.*"

Magnus worked her hips, setting a hard, fast pace that I was happy to meet. I had no desire to hold back. I hammered in her, frantic and desperate.

She dug her fingers into my back and her feet into my ass, sending spikes of need spearing through me. Her breathing grew more stuttered. More fractured. She cried out when she came, clenching around me and milking me.

I couldn't draw this out anymore. I wanted to. I wanted to stay buried inside her for hours and feel her tight, slick warmth engulf me.

My body had other ideas. I came hard, spilling inside her, thrusting the entire time and not wanting to stop even when I was spent.

The edge finally softened, and we slowed to a stop. But we leaned against the tree, her wrapped around me as we caught our breath.

"I promise this will last longer next time." I pushed the words out when I could speak again.

Magnus let out another one of those amazing laughs. "Endurance isn't everything."

"In that case, I promise to make you come more." Because there would be a next time. And another after that. And another.

"I have a hard time arguing with an oath like that."

I slipped out of her, and lowered her to the ground. I wasn't ready to let go. The way she leaned her weight into me even after she was steady on her feet made me think she wasn't ready to either.

"In a way this is terrifying." Magnus sounded like speaking the words was difficult. "The last time you and I were together, it felt a lot like this. Outside. Quiet."

And then Vidar showed up. That was what she'd told me before.

I wanted to soothe her, but wasn't sure words were adequate. That wouldn't stop me from trying. "He's not here now."

Magnus tugged me closer, until my weight pressed her into the tree. "I wish I knew how to help you remember." She kissed me.

The gesture was sweet. Soft. Enticing.

Infinite images slammed into my brain like a freight train, and I jerked away with a grunt, my eyes flying open.

I remembered *everything*.

Magnus gasped and whimpered.

I needed to claw my way through the past to get back to her, in the here and now. There were so many memories, though. The redhead from the painting wasn't real. Saving Magnus from the edge of death was. Meeting her when she woke up. Falling for her.

I remembered why I walked away from Bragi, so many years ago.

Magnus's scream yanked me out of my head, and fragments of rock pelted my skin when the crystal around her neck shattered.

Her eyelids fluttered and shut, and she slumped against me.

"Magnus." I lowered her gently to the ground.

She was still breathing. *Thank Creation.*

Her aura. I'd never seen something like it before. She was more than just a conduit, but what?

She needed help, and I needed to get her away from Bragi. *Now.*

THANK you for coming along on this wild ride with Magnus, Bragi, and Nico.
To see how things wrap up for Magnus and her men, make sure you grab DECIMATION.

www.ingramcontent.com/pod-product-compliance
Lightning Source LLC
Chambersburg PA
CBHW030855200726
48289CB00003B/766